"I Have Nothing
But Sexual Pleasure.

"Take that, one last time, and then let us forget," Arash said.

"After tonight, never again?" Lana asked.

His jaw clenched, his eyes closed, she saw his fingers unwrap one by one from the bowl of his goblet, as though taking all his concentration.

"Aren't you forgetting something?" she asked. "I think it's a tradition amongst your ancestors, isn't it, when a woman has pleased you, to grant her some boon?"

His eyes flashed purple fire. "If there is anything I have that you could wish for, I give it to you."

"You grant me whatever I ask without waiting to hear what it is?"

His head went up and she saw the shadow of a long line of proud sheikhs behind his shoulder, men whose pride had expressed itself in generosity.

"Ask your boon," commanded Sheikh Khosravi.

She took a deep, trembling breath. "I ask you to marry me."

Dear Reader,

In keeping with the celebration of Silhouette's 20th anniversary in 2000, what better way to enjoy the new century's first Valentine's Day than to read six passionate, powerful, provocative love stories from Silhouette Desire!

Beloved author Dixie Browning returns to Desire's MAN OF THE MONTH promotion with *A Bride for Jackson Powers,* also the launch title for the series THE PASSIONATE POWERS. Enjoy this gem about a single dad who becomes stranded with a beautiful widow who's his exact opposite.

Get ready to be seduced when Alexandra Sellers offers you another sheikh hero from her SONS OF THE DESERT miniseries with *Sheikh's Temptation.* Maureen Child's popular series BACHELOR BATTALION continues with *The Daddy Salute*—a marine turns helpless when he must take care of his baby, and he asks the heroine for help.

Kate Little brings you a keeper with *Husband for Keeps,* in which the heroine needs an in-name-only husband in order to hold on to her ranch. A fabulously sexy doctor returns to the woman he could never forget in *The Magnificent M.D.* by Carol Grace. And exciting newcomer Sheri WhiteFeather offers another irresistible Native American hero in *Jesse Hawk: Brave Father.*

We hope you will indulge yourself this Valentine's Day with all six of these passionate romances, only from Silhouette Desire!

Enjoy!

Joan Marlow Golan

Joan Marlow Golan
Senior Editor, Silhouette Desire

Please address questions and book requests to:
Silhouette Reader Service
U.S.: 3010 Walden Ave., P.O. Box 1325, Buffalo, NY 14269
Canadian: P.O. Box 609, Fort Erie, Ont. L2A 5X3

Sheikh's Temptation

ALEXANDRA SELLERS

Silhouette®

Desire

Published by Silhouette Books

America's Publisher of Contemporary Romance

To the last weekend at Langton Lodge
and those who share the memory

SILHOUETTE BOOKS

ISBN 0-373-76274-7

SHEIKH'S TEMPTATION

Copyright © 2000 by Alexandra Sellers

Visit us at www.romance.net

Printed in U.S.A.

Books by Alexandra Sellers

Silhouette Desire

Sheikh's Ransom #1210
The Solitary Sheikh #1217
Beloved Sheikh #1221
Occupation: Casanova #1264
Sheikh's Temptation #1274

*Sons of the Desert

Silhouette Yours Truly

A Nice Girl Like You
Not Without a Wife!
Shotgun Wedding
Occupation: Millionaire

Silhouette Intimate Moments

The Real Man #73
The Male Chauvinist #110
The Old Flame #154
The Best of Friends #348
The Man Next Door #406
A Gentleman and a Scholar #539
The Vagabond #579
Dearest Enemy #635
Roughneck #689
Bride of the Sheikh #771
Wife on Demand #833

ALEXANDRA SELLERS,

Canadian born and raised, first came to London as a drama student. She lives near Hampstead Heath with her husband, Nick. They share housekeeping with Monsieur, a beautiful tabby, who came in through the window one day and announced that he was staying.

Alexandra loves the people, languages, religions and history of Central Asia and the Middle East. She has studied Hebrew and Farsi (Persian) and is currently working on Arabic. She is the author of over twenty-five novels and a cat language textbook.

What she would miss most on a desert island is shared laughter.

Readers can write to Alexandra at P.O. Box 9449, London NW3 2WH, U.K.

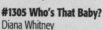

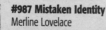

One

Winter was taking a last swipe at the mountains. A strong wind had started to blow soon after lunch, and within an hour the beautiful spring weather had developed claws. Now, wearing the anorak and jeans that had been perfectly comfortable this morning, Lana Holding was shivering, and probably it would get worse.

Static screeched in her ear again. "Nothing," she reported briefly, turning down the volume on the CB mike and tossing it through the truck window onto the passenger seat. She leaned against the truck and looked down at where Arash was tightening the wheelnuts, his left leg bent, his right leg extended awkwardly away from his body.

She could have helped with the job, but when, in his usual autocratic way, he had told her not to bother, she hadn't forced the issue. She was determined to enjoy this trip through the breathtaking Koh-i Shir mountains in spite of his presence and the jinx that seemed to be dogging them. Getting into a heated argument with Arash over changing a wheel wasn't her idea of a good time.

She sighed with ill-suppressed anxiety. "They must still be miles behind us."

Arash pulled the wrench off the last nut and straightened. "They probably have not left Seebi-Kuchek."

Seebi-Kuchek was the village where they had spent the night. Their little convoy had consisted of two trucks when they set off from the palace yesterday, one carrying Arash and Lana, the other two of Arash's staff, who had come along as bodyguards or advance men or something. Or for all she knew, their role might be just to make sure she and Arash wouldn't have to be alone.

If so, that was fine with her. Lana didn't want to be alone with Arash, either—she didn't want to be with him *at all*—but she had been impatient to get into the mountains. This morning, when the other truck had developed minor engine trouble, it was she who had suggested setting off without them.

"They can catch up with us at lunch time," she had urged. "The weather is so beautiful. I want to get up into the mountains while the sky is clear, and what if it doesn't last?"

She regretted it now, even more so because her instincts had been right. Clouds were building around the magnificent peak of Mount Shir, and soon this road would be just any old desolate stretch of road with no mountain views to entrance the eye.

Arash had agreed without a word, though she knew he hadn't liked it. They had dawdled at their lunch break, waiting for the others to catch up, but it didn't happen, and so they had gone on again. An hour later one front wheel had hit a pothole hard. Replacing the broken wheel, which had unbelievably stubborn bolts, had cost them too much time. She knew they would have to hurry if they were going to reach the village they were aiming for on the other side of the pass today.

She eyed him now. "Should we go back?"

"Your choice," Arash said, moving to set his tools into the back of the truck. He slammed the double doors. "We can go forward or back. The distance is about the same, and each way it is unlikely we will get down out of the pass before nightfall."

She eyed him in alarm. "What does that mean?"

"It means spending the night in the mountains."

Lana closed her eyes and heaved a sigh. "Why is this trip so *jinxed?*"

"I know no better than you," Arash said, in a calm voice which had the effect of irrationally irritating her.

"I know you don't know, Arash," she told him levelly. "Haven't you ever heard a rhetorical question before?"

His response was to eye her steadily for a moment and then say, as if she hadn't spoken, "Which shall it be, Lana? Forward or back?"

She could hear the suppressed impatience that was almost always in his voice when he spoke to her, and of course this stupid situation was no easier for him than for her. However much she disliked Arash Durrani ibn Zahir al Khosravi, cousin and Cup Companion to Prince Kavian, she knew he returned the compliment with at least equal force.

She couldn't imagine how he had been talked into

being her escort to Central Barakat, any more than she could understand—now—why she had accepted the situation.

She had wanted, unofficially, to be the first to travel through these fabulous, awe-inspiring mountains on the newly-built Emerald Highway which her father's money had made possible. And when Alinor—her best friend from university, now Princess of Parvan—had said that Kavian had a particular reason for wanting Arash to be her escort, had hinted that she would in this way be providing cover for a secret diplomatic mission, Lana just hadn't known how to tell her friend that the thought of making the journey in Arash's company would leach all the joy out of the adventure for her...

So now here she was, stuck in practically the most desolate mountains on the face of the earth with Arash al Khosravi, a man who got on her nerves at the best of times.

Who was still waiting for her to decide. "You're here, too," she told him. "What do you want to do?"

"Let us go on," Arash said.

Arash shifted gears for another climb on the tortuous road that, with a small chunk of Jonathan Holding's vast wealth, was being built through the mountain ranges of Shir and Noor to link Parvan with the Barakat Emirates.

He thought back to that moment when Kavi had asked him to accompany Lana Holding on her misguided pilgrimage on the still-unfinished road. Arash had never before pleaded with his prince for any favour, but he had been horrified by the request.

He had resisted in the strongest terms.

Kavi, I ask you not to ask this of me. I cannot be the one to take her through the mountains. Surely any of the others...

"As the most trusted of my Companions, Arash, you are the only one I can ask this favour," Kavi had replied uncomfortably, and Arash had realized there was more to this request than he himself had been told. "We owe her everything. How can I entrust her safety to any other?"

He gazed at his prince for a long moment as certainty crept over him. "Who has requested this, Kavi?"

"I myself make the request," Kavi said, but with a tone in his voice that belied the words. Arash opened his mouth to say that it would be worse than useless for him to make this trip, and then subsided into silence.

It was true. Kavi and the country owed Lana Holding everything. Kavi had two reasons now to bless the luck that had put him and Arash at university at the same time as Alinor, now his wife, and her friend Lana. Lana, who had turned out to be the daughter of the American billionaire Jonathan Holding, had fallen in love with Parvan, and had persuaded her father to aid the tiny kingdom in the aftermath of its savage and destructive war against the Kaljuk invaders. So this was a small sacrifice for Kavi to ask of his closest and most trusted Companion.

Between Kavi and Arash there could be no such thing as a command. Arash had not sworn to obey the Durrani, for such an oath could not be asked from one of his ancient line. But he had sworn his loyalty, and such a wish, expressed in such a way, was more powerful than a command.

On my head and eyes, Lord, he had said then, bowing formally in the most ancient of exchanges.

But he wished Kavi had laid any other mission on him.

The way Arash was pushing the truck, Lana wondered if he had changed his mind after all, and intended to get down out of the pass before they had to stop for the night.

"Mash'Allah," she reminded herself, in the way that she had learned during her time in Parvan. *Whatever God wills.* In terrain like this it was easy to remember the maxim that, whatever man proposes, it is God who disposes.

He heard the murmur and glanced over.

"Pardon?"

"I was just thinking that we might still make it down out of the pass to where we originally planned to stop if you keep it up like this."

Arash shook his head. He wished it were true. "It will be dangerous to drive after sunset."

He meant that they could not afford to risk hitting another pothole in the darkness.

Lana glanced nervously at the sky. She had been trying for the past hour to tell herself that the thick heavy clouds were moving east and the area of clear sky was no smaller than before. But they were not moving east, and the amount of blue was definitely shrinking.

He followed her gaze, but said nothing.

They rounded a curve, and he braked sharply. A spread of stones and rocks and snow had come down off the side of the mountain to spew across the road. He bumped slowly over it.

At night, without benefit of a moon, they would almost certainly have hit it before he saw it. Suddenly Lana accepted that they really would have to spend the night up here.

"What if there's a storm?" She tried to sound matter-of-fact, but she couldn't hide the note of dismay in her voice.

Arash flicked her a glance.

"Is there any protection up here?" she pursued.

He shrugged. "It is as you see."

She knew in a storm they should find cover. But here, in the remotest region of Parvan, landmine warnings were still posted prominently on both sides of the road. The snow-covered, uninhabited mountains, almost as much as the valleys, had been liberally strewn with butterfly mines by the Kaljuks in the last days of the war, before their retreat.

Anything might be a landmine in disguise—a comb, a toy, a leaf....

There were teams all over the country working hard on mine clearance: Lana knew all about it, since it was her own favourite project in Parvan.

She also knew that, except for the routes that were the nomads' regular pathways between their summer and winter grounds, including this one where the road had been built, these bleak, difficult mountains were scheduled to be the last area cleared.

It made sense to clear the valleys, the towns, the farmlands and nomad trade routes first. But it meant that even if they saw a cave or overhang, she and Arash could not just climb up to take shelter. They were safe from mines only for a few yards either side of the road, and all that had been mostly levelled to make way for the road.

A gust of wind roared down the mountainside, shaking the truck as it bumped along, spattering sand and gravel against the windshield, making her shiver.

Storm and mountain—you couldn't beat them for making a human being feel frail and insignificant.

"We can't pitch the tent if there's going to be a storm. We'll have to sit it out in the truck," she observed in a level voice.

There was silence. He did not deny it.

Lana felt the first real thrill of alarm. Sitting in a truck overnight while a storm raged with only Arash and a survival candle for company! It defied imagination. The man could barely bring himself to be civil to her at the easiest of times.

She eyed the clouds again.

"Is there going to be a lot of snow?"

It was a stupid question, which she knew as soon as she asked it. When the weather was unseasonable in the first place, who could guess? But it was just ordinary human nature to ask, Lana figured. It didn't really mark her as ignorant, but by the glance Arash threw her, you'd think she was a specimen of a species that lacked basic reasoning capabilities.

Arash shrugged. "Two inches? Two feet?"

"*Two feet?*"

"It is impossible to guess."

His voice was rough and flat, not sharing anything with her, and she had to breathe deeply to calm her irritation. She had only been making conversation to ease her nerves, and besides, he must know the ropes a lot better than she did. She'd never been up here before, but his family estates were in the Koh-i Shir mountains somewhere, so why shouldn't she ask an expert?

But what was the point in defending herself?

They always did rub each other the wrong way. It was one of those inexplicable, unfounded antipathies. Each would have been happy never to see the other again, she thought, if only one of them would leave town.

But Parvan was Arash's home, and he wasn't going to emigrate. And, apart from this short break which Alinor had insisted on, Lana wasn't going anywhere, at least until after Alinor's baby was born. And then— well, she wasn't ready yet to name a day when she would leave Parvan.

She had never met such brave, strong, true people as the citizens of Kavi's little country of mountain and desert, and here—helping, with her father's money, to put the war-torn country back together—she felt that she had found her reason for being.

"What is this, Lana, adopt-a-country?" her father had demanded in amused exasperation at yet another request for a contribution. In one of his weak moments she had convinced him to match, dollar for dollar, all the funds she raised elsewhere. "Don't I already support most of the villages and roads and wells and schools? And that mountain highway—what are you calling it, the Emerald Road?—is sucking up cash like a vacuum cleaner! What else can there be?"

"Dad, face it—if you don't spend your money on something like Parvan, what'll you spend it on? Trying to buy power, that's what. And then you won't be a great guy anymore, you'll be a monster, and everyone will hate you," she had explained ruthlessly. "And I don't want everyone in the world hating my dad."

"I'm not trying to buy power at the moment, Lana," he had told her. "I'm trying to endow a museum."

The new museum was *his* baby, and it needed lots of funds, too. But he almost always came through for her. And sometimes their interests coincided, for many wealthy Parvani families were forced into selling their ancient treasures to finance the rebuilding of their lives.

At least Lana could always make sure the Holding Museum paid well.

Kavi and Alinor and all the people whose lives she touched—whose villages and homes and farms were rebuilt, much sooner than could otherwise have been possible, with her father's generous donations and the money she raised with her fund-raising events—of course were grateful.

Only Arash stood outside the circle of her admirers. As a sheikh and tribal leader with a valley full of farms and villages to care for, he had not interfered when his people had received their share of the generosity. But as the man whose own estates and family home had suffered, he would accept nothing from her.

And although she was certain that his painful limp could be helped with surgery, he had virtually pretended not to hear her offer to finance a trip for surgery abroad.

She had never understood his reasons, and she no longer bothered to try.

She turned her head to run a look over his strong, uncompromising profile as he drove, his own attention firmly on the road. He was wearing a leather jacket and denim jeans and boots, but he looked no less a sheikh than when he was in full traditional dress.

"Will this thing drive if there's that much snow?" she couldn't help asking.

"There are too many unknowns to predict anything with certainty," he said.

"So we might end up waiting for a helicopter rescue?" Her heart sank. *And how long would that take?* she wanted to ask, but she suppressed the desire. His answer would only be another irritating refusal to guess, and she was already gritting her teeth.

"I knew I should fly," she muttered.

Arash lifted a disbelieving eyebrow. "And why didn't you?"

"Well, you know the answer to that better than I do, Arash!"

"I know only that Kavi asked me to see you safely to Central Barakat and that you insisted on coming by road."

She threw him a look. "I do know, Arash, that I'm providing cover for some secret mission to Prince Omar."

Arash frowned at the road. "I am entrusted with no mission other than delivering you safely to my cousin Omar and Princess Jana in Central Barakat."

Of course he wouldn't tell her if he was. "So why was it so important that you and no one else accompany me?" she demanded sceptically.

There was a short silence.

"But this was your own choice," he said in slight surprise.

Lana's mouth gaped. "*My* choice? What, to have you along? Why would it be *my* choice?"

"Naturally I found your motive inexplicable."

Lana turned to look at him, her eyes narrowed. "Did you really think that I had asked Kavi to force you to come with me? Kavi couldn't have told you such a thing!"

He threw her a glance, shrugging. "It was one possible explanation for something inexplicable."

"Thanks for the vote of confidence!" she snapped. "What did you think my motive was, Arash, just as a matter of interest?"

The truck slowed as his eyes briefly but electrifyingly met hers.

"I thought your motive would be revealed in time. I didn't trouble, therefore, to wonder."

"Don't hand me that!" she commanded irritably. "If you thought I engineered this, you must have had some ideas about why! What was my reason, Arash?"

She stared at him, her mind whirling, fury already bubbling up inside, and she thought how dangerous it would be to be stranded alone with Arash, of all men. She knew there was a well of resentment in her towards him.... There wasn't another of Kavi's Cup Companions she didn't like, whom she wouldn't rather have been with now.

"What reason could I possibly have for wanting to be alone with you up here in God's country?"

He made no reply. After a minute, she opened her mouth on a slow, outraged breath.

"I don't believe it!" Suddenly she could hardly get the words out for the rage that assailed her. When she spoke, her voice shook.

"What did you think, Arash? Did you think I maybe wanted to get you alone to make you an offer?"

She saw a muscle leap in his jaw and was sure she had hit home.

"What kind of an offer, exactly, were you envisaging? Just a brief affair, or was I going to go so far as to propose a mutually convenient marriage of wealth with an ancient title? Was that it?"

"It was not that I believed it. It was merely one possible explanation that crossed my mind."

"You really have to be seen to be believed!"

He slowed the truck with a quick jab at the brakes and turned to her, a blaze of fury on his face.

"You deny that such a possibility has occurred to you?"

She stared at him, the words tumbling from her lips. "*Yes,* I deny that such a possibility has occurred to me! What gives you the right to speak to me like this?"

His eyes were dark with feeling, and a shiver ran all over her. What on earth could be coming now?

He lifted a hand from the steering wheel and his finger pointed at the end of her nose. His eyes flashed violet, and the fury in his voice now astonished her.

"What gives me the right? *You* give me the right, Lana. You with your quiet suggestion that I am for sale at public tender!"

Two

It had been Lana's idea to offer a fabulous fund-raising dinner on a jet, flying guests who had paid a substantial sum for the honour overnight from London to Parvan, where they would greet the sun as it rose over magnificent Mount Shir. Then they would land at the capital to meet the Regent Prince and his wife at a palace champagne breakfast.

On board the luxuriously appointed jet, donated for the occasion by the princes of the Barakat Emirates, subscribers were also privileged to meet some of the Cup Companions....

Lana had quickly learned that Kavi's handsome Cup Companions had a drawing power second only to Prince Kavian himself, and she included them in nearly every fund-raising event. The long-suffering Companions joked that they were no better than performing bears at such times, but uncomplainingly took their turn.

It was just chance that Arash was one of the performing bears whose turn it was to appear for that particular fund-raiser—an event scheduled to last for nearly a day, and for most of which they were, of course, all captive on the aircraft.

Sheikh Arash Durrani ibn Zahir al Khosravi never failed to please women who fantasized about the Cup Companions. His charm was rough and unstudied; he never came across as practised or polished, but he had a natural charisma that had an effect in spite—or maybe because—of a sometimes impatient tongue.

Arash was tall, dark and arrogantly, powerfully good-looking, with a firmly held mouth behind a neat curling beard. His flashing dark eyes sometimes seemed black and sometimes glowed deep violet, a colour so unusual that people couldn't help remarking on it.

The fact that he had been wounded in the war with Kaljukistan and walked with a limp only added to his romantic glamour.

When in addition he was wearing the Companions' traditional state dress of flowing white oriental trousers snugly cuffed around the ankle, beaded thong sandals on strong bare feet, and a rich wine-dark silk tunic surmounted by his jewelled chain of office and his war medals—well, Lana knew it was a strong female heart that could resist.

Lana's own heart had been immunized early, so she was in no danger, but she had seen women trip over their own feet when they were still twenty paces away.

It nearly always amused her, the effect one smile from a Cup Companion could have on the donations, but it was not amusing when the Companion in question was Arash.

Probably because she didn't like him.

She also hated having to pretend enthusiasm for him with these adoring women. Arash, whose eyes sometimes seemed to hide a deep sorrow even when he smiled, was a rich source of inspiration for dreamers. She wanted to say, *Don't go anywhere near him, he's dangerous to know*…but of course she never did.

Anyone would have been guaranteed to ask how she knew. But she had never talked about it to anyone. Not even Alinor guessed that Arash and she had a past that had affected her so deeply that she still could hardly look at a man.…

"I suppose he suffered an awful lot in the war," Lucinda Burke Taylor had said with clinical soulfulness an hour or so into the flight, and Lana knew that Lucinda had sought her out for a purpose.

It was going to be a bumpy night.

Usually Lana had no difficulty enthusing about the Companions to smitten women, and the donations went up when she did. But this woman had already married two high-profile, low-income men, and a Chinese poet-in-exile was already next in her sights. It was as obvious as the day was long that she thought of these transactions in terms of purchase. His culture and brains for her money. And she believed it an equal transaction.

If she was going to start aiming at Arash…but it wasn't Lana's business. Arash would have to look after himself.

"I've heard he's the Grand Sheikh of his tribe now. It sounds so fascinating!"

"If you consider losing your father and older brother in the same war fascinating."

"Oh, of course, I didn't mean—I just meant, the whole business of being sheikh of a tribe, in this day and age! It's just so—!"

After a struggle Lana mastered herself. "He's very close to the prince, too. One of his closest and most trusted advisors," she confided.

His back turned to them, Arash was talking to someone Lana had earmarked for him. She provided each Companion with his own list of three or four of the wealthiest and most charitable people at any event. They all disliked the task, but each could be counted on to speak to everyone on his list. And usually a good proportion of Arash's targets made donations afterwards.

"And he's not married, right?"

The gunsight eyes followed as Arash and the guest unconsciously moved closer to them. Lana gritted her teeth.

"Not married, and hasn't got a bean," she heard herself say flatly.

The woman's eyes brightened at this information.

"Really?" She turned to fix her gaze on Lana, who had to consciously refrain from ducking. "Do you mean he's—" Her voice dropped to a confidential murmur. "Is he looking for a moneyed wife?"

It would be husband number three for her, and incidentally would mean sinking the fortunes of the dissident poet, but why not? Arash's estates were in ruins, and just because he wasn't accepting any from Lana didn't mean they didn't need an injection of cash.

It wasn't up to her to guess whether he would consider an offer or not.

"Might be worth putting your bid in," Lana said, glad that the other woman was apparently deaf to irony.

Arash's gaze met hers briefly across the space that divided them. He had heard some of the discussion. But instead of sending him an apologetic look, as she would have with any of the others, Lana merely raised her eyebrows in a shrug and shepherded Lucinda in his direction.

"Your Excellency…" she began, giving full weight to his title because of the impact it had on most Westerners. But the way Arash eyed her she knew he suspected her of irony.

Well, to hell with him. He knew nothing about her. If he had known her at all, he would have understood that he could take her father's money without obligation.

"…may I present Lucinda Burke Taylor?"

Maybe Lucinda would have better luck. Maybe Arash would be more comfortable with a cash sale. Maybe that had been her mistake. She hadn't asked for anything in return.

Lana frowned. *Mistake?* The only mistake she had made with Arash was a long time ago, and she was far from making another.

"I was *joking!*" she said now.

"You were not joking. She came to me as one who comes to assess a horse. She wanted to count my teeth!"

"I know she did! Don't you know irony when you hear it?"

He glanced at her. "And Miss Burke Taylor—did she know irony when she heard it?"

"I can't help it if she was too stupid to get my point. You've dealt with enough stupid, greedy women. You couldn't have had any trouble with her—she wasn't up to your weight at all!"

"Thank you." He bowed ironically over the wheel.

"But Lucinda's not the point now, is she? Where do you get the jump from Lucinda to me?"

"You?"

She breathed deep, trying to quell the irrational fury that consumed her. "Even if you thought I was serious, you have no grounds for suggesting I would want to put in a bid myself. No grounds at all!"

To her surprise, he braked and pulled over to the side of the road. He slammed the gearshift into Park and turned to her.

"What are you talking about? Why do you make so much fuss about a simple mistake?"

"I'm talking about you saying I engineered this trip so I could make a pass at you!"

He stared at her. "Are you crazy, Lana? I have just told you—"

She overrode him. "It's been a long time since I threw myself at you, Arash, and if it is not already obvious, let me make it one hundred percent clear—I am not likely to do it again!"

"You did not throw yourself at me," he said. "You offered yourself to me from compassion, the way a woman does when a man is going to war and may never come back."

"Is that what you thought?" she asked bitterly.

"Is it not the truth?"

She blinked slowly, her eyes clouding. Was it? Was

that what had motivated her? She could hardly remember now, but she supposed she must have had some reason for such crass stupidity.

"Maybe," she said. It would explain something, anyway—the thing that had always mystified her. Why had she thrown herself at him when now it was so obvious they were incompatible and didn't like each other? Just out-of-control hormones?

She sighed. "It doesn't matter now, does it?"

"No, it doesn't matter now."

"And just to set your mind at rest, Arash, in case you really are afraid it might happen again, it is just possible I might be reduced to buying a husband for myself—"

"I did not—"

"But never, in a thousand million years, would I ever consider making *you* an offer, Arash. So if you were thinking that was the reasoning behind my offer to help you rebuild your palace or your valley or anything like that, you can relax."

"I have—"

"I didn't want you to come on this trip, I was blackmailed into it, and I would have flown when I discovered you were going to be my escort, only Alinor as good as begged me not to. I have no desire ever to be alone with you, for any reason whatsoever!"

"I understood this before," he said, not without humour. "You have been at such pains to make it clear that you regretted that night, Lana, that even a stone statue would have the message by now. So I know that you do not believe what you are indignantly pretending to believe, and that you know very well that what was in my mind was no more than that Lucinda Burke Taylor had asked you to open certain negotiations for her."

Heat rushed up under her skin, and she was filled with angry shame. Oh God! What a fool she was! Of course he would never imagine…what the hell had possessed her to accuse him of thinking such a thing? It was the last thing he would think. They couldn't stand each other! She must be going crazy. Mountain air did that to some people.

"I am sure that Lucinda Burke Taylor handles her own negotiations. She must be quite polished by now," Lana muttered, bending her head to conceal her embarrassment from him.

Arash laughed, and from the corner of her eye she watched the smooth movement of his throat and smiled herself. However angry she got with him, it rarely lasted. They did have that.

There was a moment of silence while she abruptly took in the fact that they were not moving.

"Why are we stopped here? Why aren't you driving?"

He leaned forward, resting his arms over the steering wheel, and gazed out at the weather.

"We have a choice to make," he observed.

A huge gust of wind hit the side of the truck, seeming to suck the warmth out of the little cabin, and she shivered. Looking out the window, she could see lots of rock, but nothing that offered real protection.

"What choice? Is there someplace nearby where we can get under cover?"

He lifted a hand and pointed out the window beside her. "That way," he said. "It's a long trek."

She turned and stared at the rocky landscape. "What—cross-country? But what about landmines?"

"There's another mule train route here, leading to a

valley. It has been cleared by your teams. It's a long way down the road to the next such track. It may be best to make for the valley. I think it is going to be a severe storm, Lana. High winds and heavy snow. It will not be safe to remain in the truck. There may be avalanche.''

They both automatically glanced out at the snow-covered slopes, as far up as they could see. The clouds were low, dark and increasingly ominous.

"Do you mean it's going to be a blizzard? But Arash, what if it starts while we're walking?''

"That is only more reason to hurry.''

"But we might wander off the route! We could get blown to bits.''

"I know the landmarks. Whatever else happens, we will not stray from the path,'' he said briefly, without emphasis. They were both silent as they considered the other fate that might befall them, caught without shelter on a mountain at night during a storm.

"We have a mountain survival kit in the truck.'' He seemed to come to a decision. He lifted his hand to the key to shut off the engine. "We must hurry.'' He opened his door and got out.

Another gust of wind smacked at them. Arash staggered under the blast.

"Arash…'' she began, but he was already at the back of the truck, opening the doors and rooting around amongst their supplies.

"Dress warmly,'' he ordered. "Put on everything you can. More than you think you need.''

Well, it might be preferable to stagger through the mountains than sit in the truck with Arash waiting for the storm to hit. But she hated listening to him give orders as if he were an army sergeant and she a recruit.

"Thank you for that advice," she muttered, to the dashboard.

She stepped out of the truck and instantly began to shiver in the icy air. He was right—her jacket and jeans would get her nowhere. She would freeze to death if the temperature dropped much further.

Her short red curls were lifted and blown flat against her head; even her eyelashes were caught by the wind.

Her jacket billowing, she staggered to the back of the truck, where Arash dragged out the bag she pointed to and dropped it at her feet. Lana bent down and started pulling clothes out of it. She hadn't packed for cold weather; she was heading to the desert, after all. She had few suitable things. But layers were the warmest way to dress anyway.

She quickly grabbed out sweatshirts and jerseys, a pair of sweatpants, socks. Then came a couple of pairs of leggings. She gazed at them in surprise, suddenly remembering having packed them, paused for a moment, then tucked them back into the case.

"Put them on," Arash commanded her.

She glanced up. She had thought he was fully engaged, but apparently he had time to watch her.

"Put them on," he repeated in a voice that brooked no argument. Another wind slammed into them, smashing one of the doors of the truck closed, rocking the vehicle violently. It was icy cold, with fingers that reached inside the cotton shirt she was wearing to count her ribs. She shivered.

"Are you crazy? I'd have to take off my jeans first! I'd freeze just putting them on!"

"You will quickly get warm again when we start to walk," he said.

She really didn't want to strip off in the middle of the road—in front of Arash—if she could help it.

"I'm sure I'll be all right with—"

"The temperature is still dropping. We have a long walk on exposed mountain."

She still hesitated, and his voice got flatter and more urgent.

"Lana, we are using valuable time. Do as I say! Take off your jeans!"

The explosion over, his words hung in the air. Their eyes met.

A muscle pulsed in his jaw. She wished they could laugh. It should have amused them. But somehow, instead, she felt heat burn up in her cheeks. Lana turned away and pulled her jacket off, reaching for a jersey.

As she pulled on all her sweaters, Arash pulled on a thick tracksuit over his jeans and shirt, then a heavy sweater and down vest, and then his leather jacket. All right for him, he didn't have to strip off his jeans, Lana thought bitterly, pulling down the zipper and shivering as she slipped the denim down over her hips.

Underneath she was wearing only a tiny pair of briefs in paper-thin yellow Lycra, and she saw Arash glance involuntarily at her bare hips and thighs before he firmly continued with his own business.

It was just male instinct, she told herself, trying to ignore her reaction to his glance. Trying not to remember the last time he had looked at her body.

Her jeans around her knees, she held down her boot heel with the other toe and tried to prise her foot free, but her feet must have swollen during the long drive—the boot was stuck.

"Damn!" she swore, wrestling with the boot for a moment before starting to hike her jeans back up.

"What is it?" Arash turned. He had dressed quickly and was packing the supplies. He held a coil of rope in his hand. "Lana, believe me, it is best if you put on everything you can."

"I'm *trying* to. I can't get my boots off!" she exploded. Now she couldn't get her jeans back up over her hips.

Without another word Arash sank down at her feet and quickly loosened the laces.

"Lift your foot," he commanded impatiently, and when she mutely obeyed he wrapped one hand around her ankle and worked the boot off with the other.

She shivered violently. It really was freezing. Hastily she stepped with her free foot on the gravelly road to let Arash draw off the other boot. She shoved her jeans down again, and he took over to pull them down over her knees and shins and off one foot and then the other.

Then she stood half naked in front of him, nothing on her lower body except the yellow bikini briefs. Lana swallowed convulsively, looking down at his dark, thickly waving hair as he lifted his head and frowned questioningly up into her eyes.

For a moment they were both silent, remembering.

"Ohhh, it's *cold!*" she cried, pretending that she had been assailed by no memory of another life, another world.

Arash got to his feet and turned to business, and Lana shook out the first pair of leggings, lifted a foot and quickly began to work them on.

When she had put on the leggings and jeans and her sweatpants she began to warm up again. She quickly pulled on her boots and jacket, tied a big silk scarf around her head and face, pulled up her hood and made the drawstrings tight. She slipped a small toiletries bag with the bare essentials into her pocket.

Meanwhile Arash had stuffed two backpacks full, and was tying a rope around his waist. When that was done he took the other end and began to tie it around her.

"What on earth are you doing?" she demanded.

He threw her a look and went on tying the rope.

"Answer me, Arash!"

His hands stilled for one moment of what looked like irritation and he looked into her eyes at close quarters. In this grey light his eyes were the colour of crushed dark violets. She could almost smell their perfume.

"I am tying a rope around your waist," he said levelly.

"I can see that!"

He shrugged. "You asked the question."

"You know what I meant!"

"The reason for what I am doing is as obvious as the action itself. What do you want me to say? If you get blinded by the storm, do you relish the prospect of wandering off the path away from me and getting lost—or worse? Do not waste time on argument, Lana! Every second counts! You must submit to me in this! If you challenge me every step of the way, we are doomed."

You must submit to me in this.

Lana swallowed. Of course he was right. He was the expert here. "Sorry," she muttered, and then turned and slipped into the straps of the backpack he held up for her. A moment later he had shouldered another one himself, larger, heavier.

"Ready?" he asked.

Together they stepped into the storm. Survival depended on mutual cooperation now. She wondered if they could achieve it.

She had gone to London to study at university, wanting adventure, wanting travel, wanting to get away from the restrictions that her father's sudden wealth imposed on her life.

Lana had been born and raised in an ordinary, comfortably-off family environment, with a father she hardly saw and a mother who was proportionately devoted to maintaining home and family. She rarely spent time with her father because his field was computers, and when Lana was about five he had taken the plunge of starting his own company.

Within ten years Jonathan Holding was almost a billionaire, and Lana's life had changed completely. She had of course enjoyed the freedoms that such wealth offered, but she had equally disliked the restrictions that it imposed.

The worst effect was in her dating life. She had only been sixteen when she had had to fight off a date rape from a guy who, when a well-placed kick had finally calmed his ardour, had drunkenly apologized and confessed that he had wanted to be able to claim he had deflowered Jonathan Holding's daughter.

He was a student at a nearby private school for boys. That night she had learned that there was a competition among the guys: the goal was to get the ''virgin's panties' of the daughter of someone famous to hang on your gym locker door. Lana Holding's panties would be almost as much of a feather in a guy's cap as those of the daughter of a high-profile movie star, who was her fellow student.

That experience had made her very, very wary. Afterwards she listened to her friends when they talked about sex, about how they had meant to resist but had been overcome by their own passion, or by a guy's, or by his arguments or bad temper, or merely by their own impatience to know what it was all about....

Not Lana. The experience gave her breathing time, and a good reason for resisting during those first cloudy, hormone- hazy days of growing up. And when the cloud had cleared a little, she had realized that she wanted a lot more from a guy than just his determination to get her underpants from her. And a lot more from herself than just her hormones crying out for relief.

She had decided to go abroad to university, where with a little luck she could be just an ordinary person again. She had taken her mother's name to become plain Lana Brooks, though at her father's insistence she had agreed to live in a building with extremely high security.

Lana had been lonely in the huge and luxurious apartment, until she had invited her best friend, Alinor, to share the place with her.

Alinor had already caught the eye of the mysterious graduate student Kavian Durran, who rumour said was an important member of the Parvan royal family. He was accompanied everywhere he went by the two Parvani friends who had come to England with him. Rumour said *they* were actually bodyguards.

One of them called himself Arash Khosravi.

Three

Lana bit hungrily into a piece of *naan*. "Where are we?" she asked, chewing.

Buffeted by howling winds, they had been struggling across rocky ground for well over an hour, and if there was a path, she certainly hadn't seen any markings.

Every step terrified her. The thought of what would happen if he put his foot on a mine made her sick with fear. She had gritted her teeth till her jaw ached. *Not him,* she had silently pleaded. *After all that he's suffered, don't let him...* She didn't like him, but she was a long way from wanting to watch a landmine blow his foot off.

But he had brought them safely to their first rest stop. "Five minutes," he had said, eyeing the sky. The snow had started to fall almost as he spoke, and a layer of powder was already settling on the ground, being blown into little ridges under rocks and against stones.

Arash had set a hard pace, and his knee must be bothering him. She knew he had been hoping to reach their destination before the first sign of snow, and he did not hide his anxiety to get going again.

"In that direction," he replied now, pointing in a direction she guessed was south, "not far from the Barakat border. Maybe twenty miles."

"And in the direction we're heading?"

There was warm soup left over from lunch, in the thermos flask. It had been filled this morning by a woman in Seebi-Kuchek, the village where they had spent the night, and although of course Lana had thanked her, she was a lot more grateful for it than she had imagined being.

They had only the flask lid as cup. Arash lifted the cup to his lips once for every time she did, but he could barely have warmed his lips for the amount he drank.

"We are heading towards a river valley. There we will find shelter."

She didn't bother to ask how much longer they had to go. They would either make it before the storm broke or they wouldn't. She nodded, finishing the last bite of her bread, and dusted the crumbs from her knees. Arash held up the cup of soup to her.

"Finish this off."

She was hungry. A long time ago, in a past of plenty which she could now hardly recognize, she might have drunk the soup without a thought. Lana had always been an exhuberant eater. She had never worried about her weight, or whether people—other women, mostly—had thought her fat. She loved food and she indulged herself.

But she never took food for granted now. Too often she had seen poor villagers produce their last morsel of food for their visitors...the generosity of the people here was the deepest she had ever met.

So she stood, looking down to where Arash sat on a rock, his right leg extended. He too was much thinner now, though every gesture still carried the promise of power. "Thanks, Arash, I've had plenty."

She saw his pupils expand, all at once, like a cat's. Then his eyes fell to the cup between his hands. After a moment, he lifted it to his mouth and drank deeply.

He held it out to her again. "The last mouthful is for you."

He had drunk less than half, but she could not argue the point further. She took the cup with a nod and gratefully drained it, while Arash with quick efficiency cleaned up the remains of their meagre meal.

He stood, drawing his right foot under him in the awkward way she was used to, and Lana unconsciously tightened her lips and shook her head. She *knew* something could be done, if not to restore full function to the knee, at least to relieve the constant pain she was sure he suffered. She had asked a couple of surgeons about his case, and the prognosis was pretty clear. Why wouldn't he let her father finance the operation?

They shouldered their backpacks in silence. "Ready?" Arash asked briefly, and at her nod stepped into the wind and started off. Lana followed as the rope that joined them lost its slack.

Her hands were cold. She had only two thin pairs of gloves, and other than drawing her hands up inside her sleeves there wasn't much she could do to warm them. Pockets were out of the question most of the way—she needed her arms free for balance.

The wind was horrible; she had never experienced such cold, strong winds in her life. Thank God now, except for gusts, it mostly came from behind. Whenever it blew into her face and her nose, terrifyingly, it seemed to suck the breath from her lungs.

They had been heading downhill for some time. More than once she was blown against Arash's back. On each occasion he stopped, firm as a rock, till she got her balance, then with a brief word set off again.

"I suppose that's a knack you get when you're raised in the mountains," she called once, but if he answered her, the wind snatched away his words.

It was funny—she didn't like him, but she trusted him. There was no one she would rather have been in this trouble with, no one she would have trusted more to get her through this.

She searched for her reasons. Because he was not a man who lied to himself. Arash never disguised his perception of reality in order to bolster his ego.

How rare that was among men.

She knew there was no one Kavi trusted more. "Arash is my right hand," she had heard him say to Alinor once. "If I only think about a thing, it is done, as if my own hand had done it."

He was as fine a warrior as any of his famous ancestors: the Parvanis were a nation of storytellers and she had heard plenty of stories about Arash's war exploits, from everyone but him.

She had nothing but respect for him as a man. She had never seen him perform an ungenerous act.

Except one.

It was a pity they couldn't like each other. But chemistry was like that, sometimes. Something primitive operating in spite of all rational process.

And she, of course, had other reasons.

They came to ground that sloped sharply upwards, and here, the vegetation having got a little thicker, the path was visible. Arash turned up a defile, and the wind simultaneously changed direction and blasted fiercely at them. The snow it carried was cold and hard, stinging her face with sudden ferocity.

Losing her balance, Lana stumbled and cried out, but though the wind seemed to steal the cry right from her throat, Arash turned and stepped quickly down to her, his hand outstretched.

She grasped it and recovered her balance, her heart beating so hard and fast that she was lightheaded for a moment. She clasped her other hand to her chest and blew out a relieved breath.

"Thanks!"

Her pack was heavy enough to have made a fall nasty. She might have broken a bone. His grip was firm, and he held her for an extra second to be sure she was safe. Her heart was still going like a drumroll.

"All right?" Arash asked. "It will be easier very soon now."

She nodded, and he let her hand go, turned and went on.

For a moment she stood frowning down at her hand. Just with that brief touch his hand had warmed her freezing fingers.

After a long struggle, half-blinded by the snow, they crested the ridge, and the world was transformed. Lana, breathing heavily from exertion, gasped at her first glimpse of what lay below.

Behind was the familiar white and grey of rock and mountain and snow, but at their feet the ground opened, as if a giant knife had cut a gash in the fabric of the earth and the two sides had been pulled apart to reveal the earth's deepest beauty in a vast, rich valley.

"But it's magic!" she exclaimed breathlessly. "Oh, Arash, how beautiful! It's like—it's like Shangri-La!"

It was green with spring growth and the early buds on numerous trees. There were neatly planted orchards in a dozen directions, as well as the wild growth of natural forests.

There were villages, and farms with the neat, centuries-old terracing she had come to expect in Parvan. There were sheep and goats freckling the fields, and their bells jangled on the wild wind as shepherds hastily drove them home.

As everywhere in Parvan, there was evidence of the Kaljuks' destructive bombs. Terraced fields were smashed, a roofless house gaped helplessly at the coming storm, sad skeletons of a burnt orchard clawed emptily at the sky.

But there were also signs everywhere that the inhabitants were rebuilding their lives. A half-finished new roof, the fresh bricks of a rebuilt muezzin tower, freshly plowed land.

Far to their right, a river cut through a rocky gorge and thundered in a massive, breathtaking waterfall down to the valley floor so far below. There it continued its journey as a river again, glistening between rich hilly banks all along the valley till it was lost to view.

At their feet the path they had been following suddenly became visible as a trail leading along the steeply sloping side of the valley down towards the river. It branched out in many directions, and she realized that this path was the inhabitants' link to the caravan route and the outer world.

A blast of wind drove more stinging snow into her face as she paused to catch her breath, and Arash said, "We must hurry to get to cover. There is still some way to go."

"Has the valley been cleared of mines?" she asked.

He nodded. "This valley was mostly spared the mines in any case, being so close to the Barakat border. The Kaljuks were afraid of bringing the Barakat Emirates into the war against them. If a pilot had made a mistake, if the mines or the bombs fell across the border…"

"I thought Central Barakat came in on Prince Kavi's side."

"Prince Omar is Kavi's cousin and mine. He fought the war unofficially. His brothers, too, sent money and arms. But to engage the Barakat Emirates officially— the Kaljuks were at great pains to give them no excuse to formally declare war."

"So this valley was luckier than some."

He twisted his head in a nod. "As you say."

"What is its name?" she asked, but Arash shook his head.

"Save your questions, Lana."

He did not take the main path, leading to the left and sharply down, but a less-defined, though still visible, route to the right, in the direction of the waterfall. High on the green slope, it seemed more of a goat track than a human pathway.

Suddenly the storm broke in earnest. The muddy goatprints began filling with snow. The pattern of the wind was visible in the snowflakes' whirling dance. Her eyes traced whorls, and spirals, and long sweeping blasts, and leaping chaos, all within the space of a few seconds.

The thought entered her mind—*the secret of life is in those patterns, if only I could understand them*. Then she blinked in surprise. She must be lightheaded from exertion and lack of calories. Or rapture of the heights.

One of Kavi's bodyguards was a walking, talking sex bomb, as far as Lana was concerned. Arash Khosravi was powerfully built, and in their many discussions about the mysterious trio of Parvanis attending the university, Lana and Alinor convinced themselves that he really was a bodyguard.

He was also ruggedly good-looking, his eyes were a deep, unbelievably sexy violet, and he exuded masculine sexual confidence.

When he looked at her, Lana never felt that assessment in his gaze that she had learned to hate from men, never felt that question hovering in the air between them: *Could I?*

Arash's sexual assessment was very different. When he looked at her, she seemed to hear a voice inside her head, saying, *You have never wept with pleasure. I will make you do so.* Or *You have never been given all that you need. I will teach you how much more you need than you believe now.*

She was sure he didn't guess how far she was from the experience of real sexual pleasure.

When Kavian and Alinor started to date, Lana and Arash of course were often thrown together. Up close she had found him breathtaking. Mysterious, elemental. He was so different from the men she knew.

Even the way he carried himself was different. He walked as though the air were his own, and with every step his body seemed to restate a deep connection with the earth, as though his movements were part of the earth's breath.

For a while she had been convinced the deep, almost primitive attraction she felt was mutual. She had told herself that Arash was choosing his moment. She imagined that he was deliberately building the intensity between them, increasing their anticipation.

She wished she had the courage to tell him her anticipation didn't need any help. She had never felt such powerful sensual excitement in a man's presence. Looking forward to the day Arash would make his move, she would burn and freeze and melt and shiver all at the same time.

Maybe, if she had not been so totally inexperienced, she might have been more confident that he would welcome some move from her. But he made her so nervous. What if she was imagining it all? What if her hormones had just made her sexually crazy?

The day drew nearer and nearer when he would go home....

Each day her heart ached a little more. Each day she thought, *This will be the day*. Each day she trembled when he was near.

And then the impossible arrived. Kavi and Alinor were leaving for Parvan the next day, and Arash was going with them. And with a deep sense of shock, Lana had realized that he was never going to make his move. And she might never see him again.

That night, at a farewell party at Kavi's place, a little drunk—a little drunk and a lot desperate—Lana had stared across the room at Arash Khosravi where he leaned against a wall watching the proceedings, and knew that this was her last chance and that she could not let him go without a word....

She heard the introductory strains of a slow sexy song and, swaying across the room to where he stood, had slipped her body into his surprised hold, and her arms around his neck.

"Dance with me, Arash," she breathed softly, smiling. "You're going home tomorrow. Dance with me tonight."

They struggled along the path that Arash chose. The evening closed in, and below them, all along the valley, lights came on in villages and isolated farms. And still they walked, the path dropping very gently as it proceeded around the valley's slope, leading closer and closer to the waterfall. Its comforting rumble grew steadily louder, even against the blast and thunder of the wind and the thickening fall of snow.

She realized, after a while, that he had some specific goal in mind, and knew exactly how to get there. Several times before the snow got deep enough to cover all trace of the track, she noticed other tracks branching off, leading perhaps to this or that distant flickering light or cluster of lights marking a farmhouse or a village. But he always chose his path without hesitation.

Ahead of them there seemed to be nothing but shadow and the sound of the falls. Yet he moved sure-footedly, not pausing to take his bearings.

Then at last, just before evening darkened into night, when she thought her fingers and her nose must be black with frostbite, he stopped. The snow whirled, and Lana gasped as a white-grey wall loomed up in front of her.

A door creaked, and Arash led her through into a

courtyard. There was less protection here than she would have imagined from the height of the wall, but the reason became evident when another gust swept aside the falling snow to reveal massive damage a little further along.

"Ya Sulayman! Ya Suhail!" Arash called, but his voice was eaten up in the roar of the storm.

There was no light anywhere.

"Is there a house?" Lana asked, peering around her. The wall was fairly typical, a kind she had seen before. It probably surrounded a large house and garden and perhaps an orchard. Generally such a place was the home of the sheikh or tribal leader, or the village chief. In her travels, finding the best projects to undertake— digging a new well here, rebuilding the mosque school there—she had often been offered the hospitality of such homes.

So it was likely that Arash had brought her to the house of the local sheikh. But it was strange that there were no lights. The house of a village chief should be full of people and lights, and, in weather like this, the courtyard and even some of the rooms might be crowded with animals. She wondered if it was even still standing.

"Yes, there is a house," Arash responded, after shouting again and receiving no reply. "What is left of it."

He moved forward, and she had to follow. Then, as they got closer, the snow briefly cleared, and she caught a broad vista of a once palatial, but badly damaged house. It had obviously been the home of an important sheikh. Probably the tribal leader of the whole valley, with a pedigree going back centuries.

Even half shrouded by the storm and cloaked in

night, the ruin made her shake her head in sorrow. It must have been a beautiful place, built on several terraced levels up the hillside.

As they walked she saw the intricately patterned paving stones under her feet, broken now, and a dry channel said that a spring had once made its way through the garden. There were the remains of delicate archways and, just visible on the far side of the flat roof, an intact dome.

Although there were some signs of industry—a neat pile of new bricks, some boarded-up windows—no extensive repair seemed to have begun.

Arash led her towards a doorway and pushed open the door, and she followed him inside, out of the wind's icy blast.

He shoved the door shut against the wind. They stood for a moment in total darkness. Catching her breath, she felt him fumble with something.

"Didn't we bring a flashlight?" she asked, and found that she was speaking in a whisper.

"One moment," Arash said, in a normal voice, and just then a match flared and she saw his hand reach for the glass chimney of an oil lamp on a small shelf just above her eye level at the doorway.

He lit the wick and replaced the chimney, then poked the small metal match back into the little box and restored it to its place behind the lamp. Dimly she wondered how he had known where the flintbox was in the darkness.

They stood looking around a large shadowed room. There were windows in one wall, a rug covered a doorway leading off the wall opposite the door they had come in by, a tiny arch opened in another. The room was intact, untouched by any bomb damage, and Lana was warmer just by virtue of being out of the wind.

She gratefully stripped off her gloves and began to rub her freezing fingers as she looked around.

There were rugs spread thickly on the paving stones, a large pile of cushions, a low square table, a carved sideboard, and a big bronze charcoal brazier in one corner.

These were evidence of wealth and an important family fallen on hard times, like the house itself. Country people, and even many city people in Parvan, sat and ate their meals from a simple cloth spread on the floor.

In the corner was a folded stack of quilts on a traditional *korsi,* so they slept as well as ate here, at least in cold weather. It seemed the actual living space had shrunk to this one room.

She blew on her hands and held them to her cold nose while Arash called again and got no answer.

"I guess there's nobody home," she said.

"No," said Arash.

"Do you know the master of the house?"

"I am the master of the house," he said, bowing his head in the traditional greeting of his people. "Welcome to the ancestral home of the al Khosravi."

Four

———

The lamplight revealed some kindling wood stacked in a corner and charcoal in a metal scuttle. Arash dragged the bronze brazier over to the arched doorway in the opposite wall, lifted the rug that hung there and hooked it open. Then he began to lay a fire in the brazier.

The room was cold but not chill, and Lana wondered who was living here now, and when they would return.

There was a second oil lamp on the low table and she wordlessly knelt to light it before starting to unload food from their backpacks to create the meal they were both hungry for. Too late, she wondered if she ought to have asked permission.

It was a strange and disorienting experience to have been brought to his home so unexpectedly. Since she had come to Parvan, Arash had made it very clear he did not intend to renew any friendship with her. Refusing money was only part of it.

After an initial period of hurt confusion, she had learned to respect his boundaries—if respect was the word. She carefully avoided anything that might be construed as pushiness.

So although she had funded projects in this valley, she had never visited it. She had made a paper decision, or sent one of her team. She hadn't even known exactly where the valley was situated. She realized that she must have avoided even seeing the name on a map.

The Valley of Aram.

No, not avoided. Why should she care where Arash's home was? There were lots of valleys she hadn't been to, lots whose names she wouldn't recognize. It was only chance that this valley was among them.

Perhaps she was picking up some mood from him. Maybe it bothered him having to bring her here. She was sure only the strongest necessity could have forced him to do it. Looking back to that moment in the truck, she imagined he had made the decision with some reluctance.

And that might have nothing to do with her. Maybe that was just because it hurt him to see his home. Once so beautiful, now a ruin.

Yet it still had something.... Lana paused for a moment in her labours and looked around, like an animal sniffing the air.

"What is it?" Arash's voice invaded her thoughts.

"I don't know," she said slowly. "It's just…this place."

He was quiet for a moment. "Yes?" he prompted, when she didn't speak.

"I don't know, it's just got…it seems ridiculous to

say it, when it's been bombed, but it has such a peaceful feeling. The air seems different here. Or something," she said, laughing a little because that kind of imagining was really unlike her.

But Arash did not laugh. He nodded. "It has always been so. That is perhaps where the valley got its name."

She remembered suddenly, and smiled. It meant two things, he had told her once: in Parvani it meant the Valley of Tranquility; in Arabic, the Valley of White Antelopes.

"Have you been here very much since…have you been here recently?" she asked, on the thought.

"Twice in the past few months, for brief visits."

In a little rush of words she asked, "Do you mind my being here?"

He looked at her thoughtfully. "Mind? Why?"

Sorry that her voice had given expression to her thoughts, she shrugged.

He let the silence go on just long enough to underline it. Then he said, "I do not mind bringing you to my home, Lana."

In the handsome carved ebony sideboard that looked as though it had been imported from India in some previous century, Lana found dishes, cutlery, sugar, salt and pepper, everything neatly stacked and clearly in recent use. There was a woman's hand evident everywhere, from the high polish on the sideboard and the bronze charcoal brazier to the clean patterned cloth covering the low table.

"Who lives here now?" she asked.

"Two of my father's servants."

When the fire was going, she saw his wisdom, for most of the smoke from the brazier was drawn out through the doorway. Arash stood up, picked up his flashlight and a tin pail that stood on a small stool near the door. He disappeared out the doorway.

A warm, glowing comfort seemed to settle on the room, emanating from the two circles of lamplight and from the broad flickering fire in the brazier which sent odd moving shapes around the walls through the carved patterns in its lid.

Lana breathed deeply, absorbing the deep comfort for a moment, before getting up and moving to the stack of cushions she saw. She began to spread the cushions on two sides of the table.

When he returned with the pail full of water, Arash's hair was thick with snow.

"What's it doing out there?" Lana asked.

There was a wooden dipper on the stool and he set down the pail and put the dipper into it.

"Snowing very heavily, and a strong wind. There is a toilet. Shall I show it to you now?"

With a nod she followed him out through the curtained doorway into an adjoining room which, though she could see little detail in the flashlight's glow, seemed to be stacked with furniture. A hole in one corner of the roof let in a very cold draft and snow was drifting across the tiled floor.

Diagonally across the room there was an opening, and once through this they entered a passage. A couple of doors along, Arash stopped and opened a door.

Inside, the first thing she saw was a bucket, and her heart sank. Then, to her relief, the light brushed over a typical Parvani toilet—the white square of enamel on the floor, with a hole in the centre and two foot-shaped patches either side of it, that she had already grown accustomed to using.

Above was a cistern with a chain, but Arash said, "The water supply is damaged. There is a pail of water for sluicing."

Then he handed her the flashlight and left her.

It wasn't easy to use a typical Parvani toilet when you were wearing briefs, two pairs of leggings, a pair of jeans and sweatpants, but the icy air added impetus to her efforts. Lana was soon back in the warmth.

The fire had died down and stopped smoking, and the brazier had been moved over to within reach of the table. The carpet over the doorway was down, to keep the heat in. Arash's jacket was hanging up and his boots were by the door. He was filling a kettle as she entered, and he set it to boil on the brazier.

She moved over to the coat hooks and slipped out of her own jacket and scarf and boots. She stretched gratefully.

"Oh, that's better!"

A huge sack of rice was leaning against the sideboard. Arash took a cooking pot from a shelf high on one wall and began measuring rice and water into it, then sprinkled some salt in before kneeling to place it beside the kettle.

A charcoal brazier was really a miracle of engineering, as Lana had come to appreciate during her time visiting the countryside of Parvan. It would cook their food and provide heat, and because they were burning charcoal there would be little smoke.

This one was also beautiful to look at. The elaborate, handcrafted design that decorated it and sent haunting shadow patterns onto the walls probably meant it had descended in a wealthy family for generations. When a sheikh had commissioned such a thing from the best craftsman in an age of excellence, succeeding generations were not hasty in replacing it.

Rousing herself from her reverie, Lana moved over to sink down on the cushions by the table. Seeing him against the background of his own home, she felt her curiosity in him stirred. She didn't usually let herself think much about Arash, though she felt no such inhibition with the other Cup Companions.

"Were you born here?" she asked, when he had adjusted the pots on the brazier and relaxed back on the cushions that were kitty-corner to where she was sitting. As always, he sat with his right leg stretched out.

"Yes," he said.

"In this house?" she pressed.

He picked up two of the pieces of *naan* which she had placed on the table and reached over to balance them carefully on the handles of the brazier to warm.

"Where else?" His dark eyes moved to hers. "This is my home and the home of my family for many generations past. My ancestors were born here and *insh'Allah* my own son will be born here."

A little ripple of irritation scraped down her spine at his words.

"And where will your daughter be born?" she asked dryly, and knew only when she spoke that was not what she had wanted to say.

He gazed levelly at her. "I spoke of my son because I was speaking of his inheritance—as occupier of this house and as sheikh of the tribe of Aram. If God wills, I shall have many sons and daughters. But it is my eldest son who must inherit."

"What if you don't have a son?"

She didn't really know what prompted her to try to provoke him. Maybe just what she had feared if she was too much alone with him—a bubbling up of some nameless, long-held resentment.

When Lana had come to Parvan in the aftermath of the war and, deeply moved by what she saw, had poured her father's money like balm on the bruised and hungry land, of course she had been glad to meet Arash again. Of course she had been glad he had survived the war.

But when she tried to say so, he had looked at her gravely, as if he scarcely remembered who she was but was determined not to let her capitalize on their previous acquaintance.

Well, as if it mattered. Arash was alone in holding her at arm's length. There wasn't a Parvani citizen in the length and breadth of the land who wasn't half prepared to turn Lana Holding into a saint, among them Arash's own people.

"La-na!" they would cry, when she climbed out of a truck or helicopter or down off the back of a horse or mule, recognizing her by her curling red hair and creamy skin even if they had never seen her before, because her fame spread from valley to valley faster than her transport. "Lana!"

She soon learned that in Arabic her name meant, "he softened". For many, the "he" in question was "God," as in "God softened his anger towards us and sent us balm for our wounds." For everyone it meant that the horror of destruction was relieved by her generosity.

And the Parvanis were a people who understood generosity.

"Lana's team" would enter a village or a valley or

a field, and work for a time, and then the evil "butterfly" mines lurking in houses, in wells, in fields, in schools, mines that might otherwise have taken a foot or a hand or an eye were gone, and the people could return to the land, their homes and schools and lives.

A chief would write a letter about an irrigation system which had been deliberately destroyed by the Kaljuks, and Lana would come with her experts and find a way, and the money, to restore it. She had imported planeloads of seed and distributed it in time for the spring planting, a crucial step to recovery for the farmers, for whom the war had broken the cycle of planting and harvest. Schools and mosques everywhere were being rebuilt.

She tried never to impose, nor simply to give charity, but to find ways to help people help themselves within their own priorities. She discussed and negotiated, so that the people themselves decided what was best for them. Villages got teams of mules, perhaps, or flocks of sheep and goats, to be shared among all.

Her donations helped the many women whom the war had made widows to start herb farms, or simple factories for the manufacture and export of carpets, textiles, ceramics or other handicrafts, that they had previously produced only for their own use. In the prettiest and most historically interesting areas, they opened small tourist guest houses.

All this meant that women could earn the money to feed their families rather than be dependent on continuing handouts. And her connections abroad often guaranteed these products a market.

Parvan was beginning to thrive again, and everyone said it couldn't have been done without Lana.

Arash resolutely stood apart. His refusal to accept

any money from her various funds had always been incomprehensible to her, but of course it had never really affected her. It was his loss, not hers.

Now she was here, and could see the ruin of this once-proud house with her own eyes. And the thought that he would not compromise with his dislike of her even for the sake of restoring this beautiful estate was sharply painful.

And so, very human, she said, "What if you have no sons?"

His face closed, his jaw clenched, and he turned away from her to see to the warming bread. He carefully turned over each piece.

"If I have no son, then there will be no one to inherit the land and title," he said. "No one to carry out the sheikh's duties among the people."

His voice scarcely disguised a deep pain. She had never heard that note in his voice before. She realized that in this he was deeply, painfully vulnerable.

Lana closed her eyes, biting her lip. Her desire to hurt him had been unconscious, a basic human reaction to being hurt herself. Too late she remembered his father and elder brother, both lost in the fighting. For Arash and the people of Parvan, most of the old certainties had been wiped away.

This was not the time or place to challenge the law of primogeniture.

"I'm sorry, Arash, I didn't mean…"

"But that is a long way in the future," he continued, as if she hadn't spoken. "There is much work here to occupy me before I can think of taking comfort in a wife and family."

She glanced around them at the pitiful remains of his heritage.

"What—restoring this house, you mean?" she asked.

"This house, and the lands, and the flocks, and the valley, and the people's livelihood," he agreed.

"Are you saying you won't get married till all this—" she waved a hand, "—is rebuilt?"

"A man does not marry until he has something to offer a wife."

The charcoal brazier was hot now, shedding a very welcome warmth and a comforting red glow around the table. A pot was starting to simmer.

"Don't you think that a woman who loved you would want to share in the rebuilding with you?"

Arash gazed at her, but his dark eyes were without expression.

"A man does not marry unless he has something to offer a wife," he repeated woodenly.

Lana blinked at him.

"Are you serious?"

"Why not?"

She shrugged; it wasn't her business at all. "Well, where I come from, if a woman loves a man she doesn't wait around till he's paid the mortgage."

His eyes bored into her, his face shadowed in the flickering lamplight. She had the feeling that some of his inner control had slipped, and that she was seeing a part of him that he had been keeping hidden.

"You, of course, will not have to wait for a man to do so. You are in a position to pay the mortgage yourself."

Angry heat burned her cheeks. "What's your point? That any man will only love me for my father's money?"

"I am not such a fool," he told her flatly. There was

an expression in his eyes that she couldn't fathom. She stared as if locked by the beam, and licked her lips. Did that mean he himself found her attractive? But in that case, why...

"Well, what is your point, then?" she demanded, ruthlessly breaking into her own train of thought.

She looked away to fiddle with the intricately chased salt pot in the warm circle of lamplight, carefully aligning it out of the shadow of the matching silver sugar *qadron* so that the light glinted from its highly polished surface, as though that were an important task.

"Your father's wealth insulates you from the ordinary necessity of men and women, Lana."

"I don't think so." Ashamed of her weakness, she lifted her head and gazed deliberately into his face.

He raised his eyebrows, and she explained, "The ordinary necessity between men and women is love, and a commitment to the future. Whether two people are in this valley contemplating a bombed out ruin, or in Los Angeles trying to buy a place with a second bedroom for the baby, or in a mansion trying to book a slot at the best school, it's always going to be easier when the work is shared, isn't it?"

"This may be true where two people choose their own future. For me it is different."

"Why?"

He had spoken as though what he said was the final word on the subject. He looked irritated at being pushed.

"You think love should conquer all, Lana?" he asked dryly.

"I think I wouldn't want the man I loved to think the way you're thinking, and not many women would."

"In a situation like this—" he lifted a hand to indicate the house "—that will require many years of labour before it is habitable again, should a man ask a woman to marry him, knowing that he will be at hard physical work every day, from sunup to sundown, rebuilding all that his ancestors have built over centuries and has been destroyed?

"Should he offer a woman he loves a husband she would see only when he was racked with fatigue and frustration, too tired even to talk with her, too poor to offer her beautiful things to decorate her beauty before her youth was over? What would you think of a man who asked such sacrifice of your own youth?"

She rubbed the tip of her nose pensively. "I guess I would expect to work beside him, Arash. We could always talk while we were repairing the dry-stone walls or feeding the livestock, couldn't we?"

"I cannot ask a woman to help me in a task that is mine alone," he said, as if that argument were obvious.

"But didn't you just tell me that your son will inherit?" Not waiting for his reply, she went on, "Excuse me for pointing out the obvious, but that son will be your wife's child, too. Why shouldn't she help build an inheritance for her child?"

She waved her hand to indicate the place around them. There was a tension between them now, and she realized vaguely that it was not new.

He did not reply. "Are we talking about a real woman here?" Lana asked. "I mean, there is someone who is waiting for you to do all this work?"

He shook his head. "Once I thought to marry the woman of my choice. But the war ended that for me."

She snapped, "Well, more fool you, then."

His eyes flashed with outraged masculine fire.

"Do not call me a fool, Lana," he returned, very evenly.

"I'm sorry. But are you telling me that you have been restrained from marrying the woman you want because your life is not the same as it was before the war?"

There was another long pause as he gazed at her. Then, and she was sure he spoke against his will, he said, "Yes."

She shook her head. "And she's willing to put up with this?"

"She knows nothing of it."

Lana felt her jaw dropping. She tried to speak, stopped, tried again. "You didn't even tell her? What if she marries someone else before you're ready to declare yourself?"

"It will be best for her."

"Are you in love with her, Arash, or is this a dynastic marriage we're talking about here?"

"I am in love with her," Arash said simply, but his voice held the reflection of a deeply suppressed passion, so harsh and raw that she almost felt sorry for the woman who was the object of it. It would be like standing in a blast furnace if he ever let go.

Five

The pot of simmering water suddenly broke into a rolling boil and, as if grateful for the interruption, Arash turned and found tea and mint in the sideboard. He tossed some into the pot, then removed it from the heat.

"I hope Suhail and Sulayman won't mind when they come home and find that we've used their supplies," Lana said, grateful too for the chance to change the subject.

Arash got to his feet and moved through the shadowed room over to the window. He wiped the glass and peered out.

Then he turned. "They will not mind." He smiled. "Have you lived in my country so long without learning this?"

Lana shook her head. "No one could be in Parvan for ten minutes without learning a whole new definition of generosity,'' she assured him. ''Are they your father's servants you spoke of?''

''Yes. They live alone here now, as simple caretakers. I am sure they will be back soon,'' he said, but she wasn't sure whether it was her or himself whom he was comforting with the thought.

Lana blinked. ''They won't come home tonight, will they?''

There was a curious pause, as if this was the first time the thought had struck him. ''It is only a little after seven o'clock,'' he murmured, and his dark eyes seemed unwillingly drawn to hers. She could not read the expression in them.

Lana shivered all over her body without knowing why. Arash turned back to the window, but the shape of his back told her that whatever he saw was on his own mental screen.

''Arash, what is it? What's the matter?''

Was it possible he was worried that they were out there somewhere in the storm? It seemed so unlikely. The storm had certainly not come down without warning. But he abruptly moved towards the door, picked up his jacket and pulled it on.

''What are you doing? Where are you going?'' she cried.

''To find Suhail and Sulayman,'' he said, as if the answer were obvious. ''They are not young. The weather will make it difficult for them.''

''Arash, there's a village, there are farms, aren't there? You don't really think they're out there lost in this now? They had plenty of warning there was going to be a blizzard. Don't you think they're just staying put for the night?''

"Perhaps," he agreed, nodding. "Someone will know where. I'll find them."

He opened the door, and a blast of snow came in on a devil's wind. It scurried all around her, making her shiver. The flame in both lamps flickered; shadows danced wildly on the walls. Smoke puffed from the brazier.

"In this?" she cried, utterly mystified. "You'll freeze to death yourself!"

"It is not so bad yet. If they do not come home tonight, however..."

Lana jumped up. The lamp flames were almost blown out and it seemed as if light as well as comforting warmth was being sucked from the room. Now the shadows were not intimate, but sinister. She was floundering, out of her depth.

"Arash, you *can't* go out in this!"

She reached for him in her urgency, grabbing the stuff of his jacket in both hands, as if to hold him back forcibly. She almost laughed at the futility of it. He was so big, a mountain warrior. She couldn't have held him for a second against his will.

But at her touch, as if it had such power, he stopped.

Lana gazed into his eyes, her mind racing with conjecture.

"Please," she breathed. "If you go out in this, we might both die. What will I do if you don't come back?"

He lifted his hands to hers. She resisted only briefly as he made her let him go and drew her hands away from his chest.

"You are safe here," he said. Then he shook his head and, stepping through the doorway, banged it shut behind him. The lamp by the door went black, and for a second she thought it had gone out entirely. But the flame returned as if from nowhere to renew its struggle against the dark.

Lana shivered as the cold air encircled her. What on earth did he fear? Not that Suhail and Sulayman would have set off for home in this, she was sure. They could have stopped at any home in the valley and asked for shelter. If one thing was certain, it was that the two servants were safe somewhere.

She thought of the way he had looked at her, as if wrestling with something he could not explain, and she wondered if the storm, the shadows, even perhaps their conversation had triggered some memory in him.

Did he suffer from some war trauma? Lana's mother's brother had been in Vietnam. Lana had learned a lot about war trauma over the years of her growing up.

She also knew there had been a hard winter of fighting in the mountains and that Arash had been in several of the battles.

"Oh, God, please no!" she cried aloud, and made a dive for her own jacket and boots. In a fever of impatience she got into them and tore open the door.

"Arash!" she cried. The wind battered at the door to push her back into the room. Snow blasted, hard and stinging, into her face. This time the lamp gave up and went out. Swearing, Lana forced her way out into the darkness, dragged the door shut and then stood in the blinding, white-swirled black, trying to get her eyes accustomed, trying to find her bearings.

She groped her way across the paving stones with her arms fully outstretched ahead of her, buffeted by wind, groping for the wall. She touched it before she saw it, and kept one hand on it as she moved. After a few minutes, she felt the outer door under her hands and struggled to open it.

With a roar of rage, the wind tore it from her fingers, almost from its hinges, and bashed it back against the wall. Lana was sucked out into the cold and merciless heart of the maelstrom.

"Arash!" she screamed helplessly, while the wind smashed her to her knees as if she had been hit with a club. God in heaven, where was he? In a storm like this you could die five feet from your own front door! She had heard stories of such things happening, of bodies found huddled against some tiny protection only yards from warmth and life.

Kneeling where she had fallen, trying to see, to listen through the howl for Arash's voice, Lana felt the first icy drop of terror dribble down her spine. Where was the house? She could see nothing but the whirling of the snowflakes. Before, she had seen the secret of life in their wild dance, but now she knew it for the dance of death.

Still on her knees, she turned this way and that, her face lashed raw with stinging snow. Nothing. No one. Her confused senses scarcely told her which way the land sloped under her.

Desperately she shuffled forward on her knees. Was she going uphill or down?

She stopped and reached with her arms, feeling all around her for the wall. She must be no more than a few feet away from it, but if she went the wrong way for only a yard, she might never find it.

"Arash! Arash!" she screamed, and the wind sucked the very breath from her throat and threw the words away. "Arash!"

A hysterical giggle arose in her throat—was she offering rescue, or seeking it? What the hell good was she going to be to Arash even if she did find him? All she could do in her ignorance would be die with him.

But even though she was helpless in the face of such weather, she could not have left him out here alone. If he was in the grip of some traumatic war memory, he might be blind and deaf to the true reality of his situation. God alone knew what he might be seeing in his mind.

She might at least wake him from that.

"Arash!" she cried again. If she could find him and bring him to himself—Arash was a mountain man. He would bring them home safe again.

She began to pray, moving through the snow on her knees and sometimes on all fours—it was futile to try to stand—trying to shield her eyes from the burning, driving snow as she peered helplessly around her into the storm. Her hands were already freezing cold, and she could feel the cold seeping through at her knees.

"Arash!"

I am not going to let him die like this! What will the tribe do without him? What will Kavi do if he loses his best friend so uselessly? And Alinor, she loves him, too! How will they survive if Arash dies?

"Arash! Arash!"

So many people love him and count on him, and it would kill them if he died, and I am not going to let it happen! They love him, you can't let him die, everybody loves him, I…I…

"Aaarash! Where are you? *Aaaraaaash!*"

Out of the storm, without warning, something leapt on her. Something huge. She screamed crazily and was knocked flat into a bed of snow.

For a split second she lay passive, waiting for the first slash of tooth or claw that would end the storm and life and all for her. *Is this death, then?* she asked, with a crystal acceptance.

Then, suddenly, life erupted in her with violent denial.

"I have to find him!" she shrieked, lashing out wildly and feeling the blow connect. The animal—it must be some kind of mountain cat—reeled up in surprise.

"Lana!" it cried. *"Lana!"*

Arash.

"Arash? Oh, God! Arash!"

He tried to lift himself off her, but twice the wind blew him flat. Down at ground level, the shrieking howl was muted.

"What the hell are you doing?" Arash shouted in her ear, subsiding where he lay for a moment, stretched out, half on her body, half buried in snow.

The shape of each of them was balm to the other, the reminder of human existence in a bleak and terrifying landscape, and each unconsciously clung to the certainty that was the other.

"I was looking for you! Good thing you found me!"

She began to laugh as sweet relief flooded her. They were safe now. Arash would find the way back to warmth and life and love....

Funny how warm snow could seem when you were being buried in it. Down here on the ground, with the snow already drifting against them and Arash's breath hot on her cheek, Lana could suddenly understand those strange Northern stories about people who lay down to sleep in the blizzard. She would like nothing better than to wrap him to her like a blanket and...

He shouted again, but this time the wind howled and shrieked and she could not hear. Arash struggled up on one knee. In a wind like this the inflexibility of his leg hampered his attempts to stand, but he dragged Lana to a sitting position.

"Get up!" he ordered, and she smiled.

"Easier said than done, mister!"

They struggled to their feet at last, and then he took her hand and to Lana's amazement she took only half a dozen steps and then stepped through the courtyard doorway. Astonishing how close safety was. She had felt as if she was alone in the Arctic wastes.

They fought to get the door closed and bolted against a wind that was determined not to let them, and then made their way to the inner door and the room where warmth and light triumphed over death and darkness. This door, too, they closed and bolted.

Arash turned, and his hands of their own accord gripped her upper arms. Lana felt his heat burn through all the layers of her clothes towards her heart.

She could not find words for any of the thousand thoughts that tumbled around her mind. Something more than death had beckoned to her out in the storm, something even more dangerous.

And the threat of death had passed, but that other threat was still present. It was in the purple depths of Arash's eyes, in the hungry need she felt to fling herself against his stalwart body and assure herself he was real.

This was the deeper danger—that the brush of death's greedy fingers had torn away a veil. Behind that veil lurked a truth that she must not let herself see....

His hands tightened on her arms, and her breasts

rose and fell in a trembling breath. Time gently slowed for her, to allow her to perceive every flicker of his eyelash, every movement of the muscle in his jaw, the pulse at his throat that gave the bass beat to the music of her life. The flexing of his lips as they parted and firmly closed again.

She remembered another time when he had held her like this, when her life had trembled in the balance as it did now. *I have nothing to offer you,* he had said then.

And it was true.

She closed her eyes and turned away her head, and felt how his hands tightened in a brief convulsion and then slowly let her go.

They turned to the mundane task of kicking off their boots and hung their jackets again. Then they moved over to the low table, where the lamp still bravely burned and the brazier glowed attractively red.

The *naan* was burning.

The ordinary world slid into place with a small shock. Arash bent and snatched the two pieces of *naan* up and dropped them in the centre of the table. The smell of charred bread struck her nostrils with curious sharpness, as if her senses had responded to the threat of extinction with increased appreciation of the world.

As if they were grateful for the distraction from some other need.

Lana was suddenly starving.

She flung herself down on the cushions, reached for a piece of *naan* and, though it was burning hot, tore off a piece. She dipped it in the little dish of hummus she had set out.

''*BismAllah,*'' she murmured, and popped it into her mouth. The bread sizzled on her tongue and she panted quickly to cool it and flapped her hand in front of her mouth.

"Oh, that's delicious!" she exclaimed, when she had chewed and swallowed. "I am so hungry! Aren't you starving?"

Arash, standing above her in the gloom, breathed once, deeply. "Yes," he said. "I am starving."

To her relief he sat down and reached for some *naan*.

She had put out some of the food they had brought, and after a mouthful or two of hummus Arash picked up a dish of cold casseroled lamb and tomatoes and turned to stir it into the cooking rice.

He began rooting through the sideboard and pulled out spices he found there—cumin, she thought, and coriander—and sprinkled a tiny amount of each into the mix.

Lana's stomach growled as delicious scents rose in the steam, and she unconsciously picked up her fork and watched hungrily as he served the mixture onto their plates. The physical and mental strain she had been through had turned her ravenous hunger into sheer starvation.

Then, in the silence that real hunger imposes on eaters, they ate.

"Do you really think Suhail and Sulayman might be caught out in the storm?" she murmured tentatively, when they had eaten all the rice and lamb, and Arash was pouring tea into the two delicate, traditional tea glasses that sat in chased silver holders.

Arash's thick dark eyebrows went down in a dark, surprised frown. "No," he said.

She pressed her lips together, wondering if he

wanted her to make an opportunity to talk about whatever it was.

"But you were determined to rescue them."

He eyed her with dark intensity. "Not to rescue them. To bring them home."

"But why?"

There was a glimmer of deepest violet.

"You know what it was that drove me. Why do you wish to talk about it?"

She didn't understand why he thought she knew. Did he imagine Alinor had told her something?

"Well, if I do, it's only a very general guess. I thought that you might want to get it off your chest—"

"What could be more stupid and dangerous than to get such a thing off my chest now?" he said crushingly.

She wrapped her arms around her own shoulders. "Why, would it..." She licked her lips. "I mean, I really don't understand, Arash, so if you think I've been told something, I haven't."

"Told?" he said disbelievingly. "What need have you to be told? You know it."

She was mystified and uncomfortable, and mutely shook her head.

He gazed at her unblinkingly. "What is it, then, that you imagine the case to be?"

She half shrugged. "My uncle was in a war. He—afterwards, he used to have memories that he couldn't control. He'd just hear something and flash onto some horrible thing."

Looking at his clear eyes now she knew she had been wrong. There was no shadow there of the kind she remembered in her uncle's eyes.

"I belong to a warrior race, Lana. We fought as we

have always fought for our homeland. We fought to defend our people, our homes. I have wounds, like all my countrymen. But such memories as these that you speak of are for the Kaljuks, to remind them forever of the price of an unjust war.''

She nodded, mesmerized by his eyes and voice.

''But you are not such a fool, Lana.''

''It didn't fit with what I know of you. But—what else could it have been?'' she murmured defensively.

He shook his head and was silent, bending to drink his mint tea.

''Why won't you tell me what it was?''

She heard the little clink of the glass hitting its saucer.

''Why do you press it? What is it you want?'' His voice was soft with exasperation. ''We are alone here! You know what can happen!''

She stared at him in sudden, angry disbelief as a hint of the truth dawned on her.

''*What?*'' she cried. ''What exactly are you saying?'' It seemed to her that fury overwhelmed her in a rush of blind heat.

He was silent, his mouth tight with impatience as he watched her make for the cliff's edge against all his warnings.

''I don't believe it! You're saying you went out into that…that maelstrom, you risked your life—in order to provide us with a *chaperone?*''

Six

———

"**I** don't *believe* it!" Her blood was pumping with indignation so fierce she felt faint.

"What do you not believe?" he said in a controlled, level voice. He gazed steadily at her.

"What exactly are you suggesting?" she countered.

"In Parvan an unmarried man and woman do not stay alone together, Lana. You know this. Especially at night."

What a ridiculous, archaic sentiment! After all the stress of the day, this was just too much! She sat up straight, glaring at him.

"Why, exactly? Not because you might seduce me—you don't like me nearly enough for that! So, what then? Afraid I might try to seduce you?"

"Is it impossible?"

She gasped and drew back as if he had slapped her.

"Well, you're right, of course! It wouldn't be the

first time, would it?'' she replied bitterly. ''But we all learn our lessons, Arash. I've been immunized against your fatal charms now. I'm not likely to throw myself into your arms a second time.''

''I do not suggest that you will deliberately throw yourself at me!'' he said irritably.

''It sure sounded like it!''

''Only because you are ready to be angry with me.''

''No, I don't think so! I think I drew a perfectly reasonab—''

''Whatever you believed, and whether you had reason to do so, Lana, it is not what I meant! Why do you inflame our feelings in this way? Do you not see how dangerous high emotions are at such a time?''

''However high my emotions get, Arash, they are very unlikely to shift from anger to undying love!'' she said furiously.

He was silent, gazing at her, until she became uncomfortable.

''You are more intelligent than this. I will not argue with you,'' he said, struggling for calm. ''I am my father's heir, the spiritual and temporal leader of the tribe of Aram. My father's people would be deeply distressed to learn that I had brought to this valley and this house, and spent the night alone with, a woman who was not my wife. Let this reason be enough for you.''

''There's a blizzard, for heaven's sake!''

''That such things as blizzards can strike unexpectedly is the very reason why we should not have been travelling alone together in the beginning.''

''So what's your real point here, Arash? That we might forget who we are, or that your father's people will imagine that we did?''

"My point is no longer important. We are alone and we can do nothing about it. Except to guard against…"

"Yes, you've done it now!" She interrupted him without apology. "You probably saved our lives by bringing us here, Arash! What a pity we didn't just stay in the truck. We might have frozen to death by now, or be dead in an avalanche!"

"Why do you wish to anger me, Lana, by saying these unintelligent things? Ask yourself why! Do you not see what is already at work?"

She felt a buzz of awareness at his words, as if something in her was trying to speak, but another part of her refused to hear.

She said levelly, "I think your arrogance has to be seen to be believed. The people in this valley aren't so backward they—"

"My father's people do not receive television signals, but they know the difference between men and women. You have been raised to think you are above the human condition because of sophistication. Is it really so?"

"Are you trying to tell me that I'm going to be seized with uncontrollable desire for you, Arash, just because we're alone together? If so, you couldn't be more…"

His hand snapped across the corner of the table that separated them and closed on her wrist where her arm rested in the circle of lamplight. His strong, sensitive hand was dark and rough with outdoor work, and he cupped her wrist and showed her her own delicate bone structure, the skin that was pale and creamy after the long Parvan winter, as if it were evidence of something.

She stared at their joined flesh, frowning, puzzling over some truth in the image, as if it were a mathematical equation. Then, in the continued silence, she looked up.

His face was softly shadowed, the deep violet of his eyes reflecting the lamp's tiny fire. She gazed wordlessly into the double flames, and as if they gave off real heat her blood warmed and her heartbeat grew wild.

"I am a man," he said flatly. "You are a woman. Let this explanation serve."

And suddenly, in the rich, intimate shadows and the isolation forced on them by the storm—for something in her registered the snow-filled hurricane that surrounded the house, and was deeply and strongly aware that it was impossible that their solitude could be disturbed—suddenly, the primitive incantation took on powerful meaning, and leapt between them.

It was as if by naming a tiger he had produced one.

He was a man. She was a woman. It was a powerful, dangerous mixture, as volatile and as predictable as the chemical formula for dynamite.

She thought dimly, *Dynamite doesn't refuse to explode because people get hurt. If you hold a match to a fuse, it will blow up.*

Lana licked her lips nervously, staring at him, taking in Arash's being without a filter for the first time in a very long time.

He was fiercely attractive, powerful, a man of magnetic charisma. The passionate anger in his eyes and the set of his mouth contributed to the essence of pure masculinity that emanated from him, a perfume that could drown her senses, flood her reason.

She swallowed.

"And what does that mean?" she whispered.

He did not answer, only looked at her with a burning sensual possessiveness that was fanning a fire deep inside her, a volcano at her centre she hadn't even known was there. Slowly, as if in explanation, he lifted her wrist off the table, while his other hand came up to her throat.

With painful, erotic deliberation, he pushed her down against the cushions spread so conveniently behind her and leaned down over her. The flame of his eyes invaded her thighs and her abdomen, spread through all her limbs, with a focus of melting fire.

Her body and blood churned. Arash was deeply, powerfully, sensually attractive to her, a fact that she had somehow been able to wipe from her memory.

"Why did you push me to this proof?" he asked. "You knew from the beginning the risks."

"No," she protested weakly.

His fingers stroked her throat, her chin, with little sparks of excitement, and his mouth was only a few inches above hers. Shivers of yearning rippled through her, demanding fulfillment.

Only once before in her life had she felt such a wild flood of excitement, of desire, of the most primitive passion.

"I do not believe you have forgotten," he said. "Then, too, you knew how I struggled."

She could not speak.

He still held her wrist captive, pressed into the cushion beside her head. She lay in shadow. Only the tips of her red curls, tumbled around her head to reveal the broad, curving white forehead and ears like newly opened flowers, caught the lamplight and glinted as if

with their own fire. Her eyes searched his face disturb-
ingly.

"What shall we do, Lana? Shall we give in to this
sweet madness that can have no future, and then forget
again? Do you take your chances now?"

At his words her heart twisted with a pain she
thought she had forgotten. She *had* forgotten. She had
convinced herself it was all meaningless, and now, suddenly...

Lana closed her eyes to shut out his face, and turned
her head away.

"Not this time," she said flatly. "Let me up."

"I—" Arash began, then closed his eyes, and as if
he were fighting his way through glue, he lifted his
head, lifted his hand from her throat, let go her wrist,
like a slow-motion film. A cold draft brushed her.

He struggled clumsily to his feet and moved over to
the water pail. He dipped in the dipper and took a long
drink from it, his back to her.

Then he picked up the almost empty coal scuttle and
his flashlight and, lifting the carpet curtain, went out.

Silent and unthinking, Lana lay where he had left
her. She mechanically registered the presence of a
large tin bowl that the careful housewife had set under
the low table. She blinked, slowly taking it in. Then
she sat up, drawing the dishpan from its place, and put
it on the table. There was a thick bar of soap and a
dishcloth inside. She began stacking the dishes together.

A pot of water was simmering on the brazier. She
poured the contents into the washbowl, and added water from the pail. She picked up a knife and the bar of
soap. It was a thick, creamy grey oblong, one side
gouged out in a shiny curve. As she had seen women
do all over the villages of Parvan, Lana scraped the

knife along the curve, letting the flakes of soap fall into the tepid water.

She swirled her hand in the water to create a few suds. Her mind was empty. She seemed to have no past, no future, no self. She was just a woman preparing to wash the dishes. She watched her hand move through the water, sudsing the soap into a froth, as if it were someone else's hand.

"Dance?" he repeated. His hands gripped her waist, hard, and in the shadowy room his eyes had been black with a danger that thrilled her, and she knew she had not been wrong. Arash Khosravi was powerless to resist her, and the dance he had in mind now did not need music.

They danced. Slow, sinuous, second by second less aware of their surroundings, their perceptual world the limited-limitless expanse of each other. His body pressed hers, melted into hers, so that she marvelled at this new phenomenon that she was both herself and part of this other being that was both two and one....

Did he struggle with himself during that dance? She never knew. To her it was all inevitable, and when darkness enveloped her she opened her eyes without surprise to find that they had left the room, had danced down a hallway to shadow....

Kavi's apartment was on the second floor of the Parvan Embassy, a massive suite of rooms which his bodyguards shared with him. In the shadows in the deserted hall, Arash's hands enclosed her in a grasp that would have been painful if it hadn't been so thrilling, and his mouth came down and took rough, hungry possession of hers. His arms wrapped her tightly and the next thing she knew, he simply lifted her off her feet, pressing her flat against himself, and, still kissing her, was walking through another huge room, into another darkened hall....

His strength astonished her. At the door to a room he paused, and, their mouths still pressed hungrily together, she lifted her legs up to cling around his waist, dragging the skirt of her dress up around her naked thighs to free them. He opened the door and entered another suite of rooms.

Inside it was dark. Every second was measured, as if time had a weight and meaning she had never understood before. He closed the door and leaned back against it, and she let her legs slide down to the floor again, let her body flatten against his, as they still kissed.

No kiss had ever made her so passionately drunk, so hungry, so sure. The pressure of his hardened body against her made her tear her mouth away to gasp in oxygen.

He kissed her throat in the darkness. She felt his hair, his ear, his cheek under her trembling hand, and that was all she needed to know, that she was in Arash's arms. She had never been so hungry, so wild for a man's mouth, his hands....

"Lana," he said, his voice urgent and low, and she felt him grasp her arms and, a drowning man, lift his head for air. "I can offer you nothing. I have nothing to offer you."

"What?" she murmured, smiling, her mouth of its own accord planting a row of little kisses along the perfect line of his cheek, delighting in the roughness of his shadow beard, the firm line of bone.

His arms wrapped her again. He lifted his chin away from her mouth, grasping for control.

"There is no future with me, Lana. I go tomorrow, to fight a war. I will not come back. Say no now, Lana, if you hope for more than this. Say no."

She didn't believe him. His arms were tight around her with possession, and her heart told her that his need, like her own, was more than sexual.

She dropped back her head and looked at him from smiling, slanted eyes. "I'll take my chances," she whispered.

Lana had washed the few dishes and was drying them by the time Arash came back through the curtained doorway with a bucketful of charcoal, his head and shoulders covered with snow.

"How's the weather?" she asked, not to let silence fall between them after what had happened.

"The snow is very, very heavy. The wind is less fierce," he said, as if he agreed that silence was dangerous.

"I can still hear it roaring, though."

"That sound is the waterfall. You will get used to it."

She paused, taking that in. She would get used to it?

"Aren't we going to leave tomorrow?"

He looked at her without speaking, the expression in his mouth and eyes saying it for him, then immediately turned to the business at hand. There was a blackened area on the floor on one side of the room, and, using two big pads designed for the purpose, he began to drag the brazier towards it.

Lana bit her lip and for a few moments went on drying the dishes and putting them away in the cabinet.

Arash lifted the lid of the brazier and began to lay lumps of charcoal on the bright embers.

"How long, then?" she couldn't stop herself asking. She was shivering with nerves.

They exchanged another look. Of course he knew no better than she. She was just babbling.

"What will we do for food?" she asked, but it was not that fear which caused her to shiver.

"In the morning we will take stock. Tonight, we should assume that lamp oil at least should be conserved." He put the lid back on. "We must put the lamp out and sleep now."

He moved over to the corner where the large stool-shaped frame of the *korsi* was stored and lifted it to set it protectively over the brazier, while Lana obediently moved the cushions onto the rugs that encircled the patch of blackened tiles around the brazier.

Then, in a ritual that was hundreds of years old at least, together they began to spread the quilts over the two piles of cushions on opposite sides of the *korsi,* making a traditional Parvan winter bed.

There was one huge circular quilt, more than twelve feet across, all browned at the centre, and they spread that one last, over everything, *korsi,* cushions and all.

She had seen entire families sleep like this, their bodies radiating out from the brazier like spokes from the hub of a wheel. The *korsi* kept the quilt away from the brazier, so that it didn't catch fire, while the heat was kept under the quilt. With your feet at the centre, and only your head sticking out of the quilt, you slept in toasty comfort, warmed by the brazier's long-burning heat.

It had its drawbacks: if you gave in to the temptation to keep the room snug and close, you might die of carbon monoxide poisoning. But Arash hooked the rug over the doorway open, to keep a fresh draft flowing during the night, and she braved the cold again to visit the toilet.

When she returned, everything was ready in the room.

They took off only their sweatsuits before stretching out under the quilts. Silence fell without her noticing, and when she did, Lana couldn't seem to find the words to break it.

She lay down, shifting her body to force the cushions into a comfortable mould around her. As Arash blew out the fragile little lamp flame, the darkness fell over her like another quilt. She heard him settle back against the cushions, knew his feet were just on the other side of the brazier from hers.

"Good night," she murmured.

"Good night, Lana."

Then she wished she hadn't spoken, because the little exchange in the darkness seemed to underline their intimate isolation, and she wished suddenly that they could be lying closer together—side by side, for the warmth and comfort that another human body brings in times of hardship.

But she had taken her chances once, and lost.

He had led her into a darkened room and flicked on a small lamp. There was a small sofa cluster, bookshelves, and in an alcove, a bed.

Although it was decorated in the high Middle Eastern fashion, with beautifully patterned rugs and draped material swathing the walls, the room was completely impersonal. There wasn't one book, one item of personal belongings, and the stack of luggage by the door said it all.

He gazed at her for a moment of silence as she took it in, as if waiting for her to change her mind. In the morning, his look warned her, there would be no trace of him in this room....

She blinded and deafened herself to the warning, to the real meaning, and smiled at him with heavy-lidded, longing eyes.

"Make love to me, Arash," she pleaded softly.

He caught her wrist hard, and drew her towards the bed. The little alcove was decorated like a sultan's tent, with festoons of patterned cloth draped from the ceiling to cover all the walls...and he looked just like the sultan of a dream, barefoot in leather thong sandals, flowing white trousers and full-sleeved shirt, an intricately embroidered, jewelled, sleeveless waistcoat.

He drew her dress off over her head, just as she had dreamed he would when, earlier tonight, she had put on the silk underwear.... In deep green, softest, finest silk, she wore hareem pants that banded under the knee, a little bolero top that exposed her skin from breasts to hips. "Hareem pyjamas," the salesclerk had called the outfit, in the exclusive, crazily expensive lingerie shop where she had found them.

She looked like a Hollywood version of a concubine—voluptuous, curvaceous, her breasts spilling out of the confines of the top, her hips and thighs full and female. Her skin was rich cream, her red hair spilling over her shoulders and back to glow in the lamplight, her eyes gazing at him with deep sexual hunger and expectation....

Sitting on the edge of the bed, he drew her between his open thighs, and rested a kiss on her plump, smoothly curving stomach. His hands of their own accord stroked her naked back, her curving, silk-covered rump, her strong thighs…her arms, her breasts, her shoulders.

He drew her head down, reached up to meet her lips with his, with powerfully disturbing hunger tearing at him, fighting against his self-control.

He found himself kneeling on the floor in front of her, kissing her flesh above the edge of the silk trousers, slowly drawing the fabric away to let his mouth trail closer and closer…he reached up and unbuttoned the front closing of the little jacket, so that above him her full breasts burst free, and he felt the heavy weight against his palms, the tantalizing beading of the nipples that told him his touch was pleasure to her.…

Shadow and lamplight mingled and blended, silence and her cries or his murmurs were the same, male and female too were one as he drew her down onto the bed and stretched out beside her, above her, and at last, inside.…

He had never expected to weep at the moment of oneness, never hoped to see the full human expanse of tragedy and joy in one act, nor to feel that deep connection that said from this moment on he would understand the universe only through her.

He had never been swept with such deep, wild, honeyed pleasure, never cried a name as though it was the answer to every question he could ask the universe, now and forever.

She awoke in the depths of the night, not remembering the dream that awakened her. She had been weeping in the dream. Her head was swirling with distant nameless memories which she did not want to re-call.

Slowly, resistlessly, they surfaced—she had been dreaming of the night she had asked Arash to dance. Until tonight, she hadn't thought of that night for ages. She had put it all out of her mind.

The memory was sharp, strong, immediate, as if something in the darkness made her vulnerable, carried her straight back to that time. As if she had awakened inside that night again, as the person she had been then. Letting her feel again the passion, the yearning she had had, the need to touch him, to feel his arms around her, to believe that it meant something to him.

He had not guessed she was a virgin. He was big; her gasp of mingled pain and pleasure had been disguised by their mutual wild, drunken passion…and she was not experienced enough to know that he would have said something if he had known, or that she should tell him.

Only later did she understand the deep bond that had been forged between them, a bond she should have made him conscious of.…

She had fallen asleep while the birds sang their early chorus, feeling that they sang the song of her heart, with a sure sense of rightness binding her to Arash, whose firm, muscled chest was under her head, whose arm enclosed her, whose hand gripped her in a word-less message of belonging.…

She had awoken to solitude and silence. She sat up with a smile, looked around the room…and saw only her own clothing laid neatly over a chair. Her little handbag, which she had last seen on a sofa in the room where the party was held, was there, too.

The pile of luggage was gone, Arash's clothes were

gone. There wasn't a sign or sound to tell her another living being was in the world.

She flew up off the bed, dashed on her clothes, and ran out of the room and into the flat. A small group of cleaners was at work in the place...Prince Kavian and the others had left for the airport an hour ago.

She returned to his empty bedroom to search for a note, a message...nothing. She asked the cleaning staff...they had seen nothing, no paper, no message had been left.

So it was there, in the massively ornate main room of the Crown Prince's apartment in the Parvan Embassy, surrounded by sympathetic but uncomprehending strangers, that Lana had finally understood her own feelings.

Slowly, with absent steps, she had left the place, had wandered into the street, had hailed a black cab...had returned home.

There was a message on the answer phone, from Alinor. "Where did you get to? I'm sorry we never got a chance to say goodbye...."

No message from Arash, of course. And now, as well as understanding herself, she understood him.

"I have nothing to offer you, Lana..."

Love, he meant. He did not love her.

She had been in love with him. Crazily, wildly, deeply and passionately in love. With a love that, when she had finally accepted that she meant nothing to him, had nearly torn her heart in two.

Now it all came back...things she had forgotten, had forced out of her mind and memories in order to survive....

He had believed that an invasion of his country by its neighbour was inevitable—she had known that he was convinced that he was going home to fight a war. Prince Kavian had still been hopeful that it could be avoided, but Lana had watched Arash when his prince spoke of diplomatic solutions, had seen the bleakness in his eyes.

Once she had asked him what the result of war would be. She had forgotten that, too. But now she remembered as if she had asked him the question to-night.

She remembered the utter hopelessness in his expression, as if he already saw the loss of everything in life that held meaning for him.

"It means our total destruction, Lana," he had said. "We are a tiny nation and our oil reserves are not easy to access—the mountains make it difficult. Kaljukistan has much oil, and markets that the West wishes to exploit. It has also the arsenal left behind by its former Soviet masters. Who will help us in this war? Who will take our side?

"We have a way of life that is centuries old. It will be wiped out. All our wealth for generations will be mortgaged to buy the weapons we will need…we will have nothing. In the end we will have our sovereignty. Nothing besides."

Fearfully, she had asked, "But they won't win?"

"They will never win unless they kill every Parvani breathing. As long as one of us has breath Parvan will fight."

If he had given her the smallest opening, she would have said, "Let me come and fight beside you," that was how besotted she had been. She had ached for him, she had yearned to go and help to fight his war. But he had given her no opening….

She had thought of him constantly after he left,

sometimes not knowing for months at a stretch whether he lived or died. The Parvani-Kaljuki war was not a popular cause with Western journalists. She had learned then that no news was not good news. No news made you helpless, anxious, terrified that the blow might fall at any moment.

One day at university a fellow student had breathlessly told her, "Did you hear that one of Prince Kavian's friends got killed a couple of days ago? One of the blokes who was here with him?"

Her heart—her heart had clenched so spasmodically it seemed to stop the flow of life within her. She remembered the pain now with a renewal of that terrible, aching breathlessness, the ugly fear...it had showed her how wide was the gulf between hopelessness and real acceptance.

It was a dark, evil twenty-four hours before she could find out whether it was Arash or Jamshid who had died, because whichever one of them lived, whoever had died, the news was horrible, and yet she couldn't stop herself from wishing that it would not be *him*....

It was not him. It was Jamshid. Lana had grieved deeply for the handsome, laughing man, so young, so senselessly dead—so deeply that she had believed that if she did hear the news of Arash's death, she would not survive it.

If she had felt any hope that he would welcome it, Lana would have gone to Parvan then, would have found him, wherever he was, and told him...

But the war had closed the borders. With money, she probably could have gotten around that. But she did not believe he would welcome her or her love. He had told her she meant nothing to him, and he had left without one word, just to underline that message.

Jamshid had left behind a wife planning to join him as soon as the war was over. She had given birth to his child a few months after the news of his death.

"What a pity she's been saddled with the child," people said, but Lana had never said that. Never thought it. She had envied the other girl with a feverish pain, because she had her young son as a memento.

If Arash died Lana herself would have nothing. She had never heard one word of love from him. She would have nothing except the memory of those few dark hours of purely physical passion which had meant exactly nothing.

As if her dreams tonight had stripped the armour from her heart, the old raw, tearing pain lashed through her with a heightened urgency. Lana gasped for air, pressing her hands to her mouth, trying to make no sound.

What a fool she had been, to imagine that she had sealed her heart with common sense, had learned that love was a dream. Love was reality, harsh and cruel, where you had nowhere to hide, and you never woke up.

Now, when it was too late, it was all spread out for her, like a tapestry. The truth of who she was, what she felt, what she had done.

She had come all this way, begged money from her father, from friends, from strangers, worked harder than she had ever worked in her life. She had gone hungry when his people went hungry, she had wept when they suffered, she had stretched her powers and abilities to the limit to try to restore to them their lives....

Because a man who did not even like her had said one night, with heartbreak in his voice, *We will have nothing*.

Seven

The room was cold but bright when she awoke. There were thick designs of frost on the windows and she could see her breath on the air. Her nose was cold. Lana lay under the heavy layers of quilt without stirring, enjoying the warmth for a few more minutes.

Snowflakes were still falling heavily beyond the windows, a thick soft fall of flakes that seemed to mute the waterfall's roar. She lay drowsily, not thinking of anything.

In the next room she heard banging and lifted her head to peer around the mound of the *korsi,* disturbing the quilts and letting cold air into her cosy nest.

Arash was already up. Taking a deep breath to prepare herself, Lana eased back the quilts and got up.

"Ahh!" she cried involuntarily as the cold air enveloped her body. The place was freezing! She went through the curtained archway in her stockinged feet and made a mad dash across ice-cold tiles to the toilet. On the way back, she saw that the banging noise came from the high corner where the roof was damaged. Arash was outside on the roof, hammering some plastic sheeting over the hole.

Back inside the main room, she carefully folded the quilts and stacked them and the *korsi* back in their corner again, then bent to the task of resuscitating the fire. There were still plenty of embers in the brazier, and a careful laying of new charcoal would get it going again.

Just like her love. It had burned down to embers, so that she had hardly known they were there. And now she had put new fuel on the embers, and it would burn her again....

What a fool she had been to come on this trip with Arash. Why hadn't she listened to that little niggle of fear, that voice that had warned her that that way lay danger? She should have abandoned the idea of the drive through the mountains, if he had to be her escort. She should have gone by air.

She forced herself to put him out of her mind and began the search for breakfast provisions. By the time Arash came down off the roof and through the door, rubbing his cold hands, there was tea and toasted *naan* with butter and apricot preserves almost ready, but she had not succeeded in controlling her thoughts....

"Great!" he said, kicking off his boots and hanging up his jacket. "Nice and warm in here!"

Compared to outdoors, perhaps. But the brazier really wasn't up to heating the whole room comfortably in a prolonged cold spell. In weather like this, a Parvani family might spend the whole day huddling under the quilt around the hot brazier.

Arash sank down on the cushions she had placed by the table. As if reading her thoughts, he nodded his head towards the other room and said, ''There are a couple of empty oil heaters out there. We can have a look after breakfast to see if there's any fuel for them.''

''Where did you find that sheet of plastic for the roof?''

''It was already there. The wind had dislodged it,'' he answered, as she pulled the hot *naan* off the brazier with her bare fingers and dropped it quickly onto the plate she had left ready, crying, ''Ah, ah, ah!''

She shook her hand to disperse the heat before repeating the entire action with the second *naan*.

Arash laughed.

''There's a pot holder,'' he pointed out.

Lana gazed at his smiling face, his laughing eyes, and wondered how she could ever have convinced herself that she had no feelings for this man.

Now her love seemed to her to have always been there, following her close as a shadow, moving out of her vision when she turned her head, perhaps, but always there.

She had been hoping that with the clear light of day those night thoughts would disappear, like most worries that plague sleepless humans in the early hours, but all she had to do was look into his face to know that no longer could she hide behind indifference.

She had caught her own shadow.

''Arash—'' she began, then choked herself off. She bit her lip in frightened astonishment. What had she been going to say? ''I've just remembered I love you''? Just like that, as if it might be something he wanted to hear?

She had had no practice in guarding her tongue. She

had worked more deeply, convincing herself that she had no feelings. Now that that fence had fallen, there were no barriers between feeling and voice.

"Yes?"

"Do you want tea?"

"Thank you."

She poured, and they ate the simple breakfast in silence. Her mind was too full of thoughts to notice.

"How long will we be here, Arash?" she asked.

"If we find snowshoes, perhaps tomorrow we can leave." He spoke as if he hoped so. "We will not know for sure until the snow stops."

"Is there any chance we'll find food stores?" Lana asked.

"I am sure there will be something. In any case, there will be a gun and ammunition," Arash murmured thoughtfully.

"You mean you'll go hunting for our food?"

"If necessary. I want to make a tour of the house. We can check the stores afterwards. Do you wish to come with me?"

She wanted to see his home, as if some part of her whispered that she would know him better if she knew the place where he had spent his childhood and youth. She nodded, and a few minutes later they were on their feet, pulling on boots and jackets and gloves.

He led her through the curtained doorway and across the adjoining room in the way she already knew, and along the corridor past the toilet.

At the far end of this corridor was a short flight of stairs, leading at the top through another archway and into a massive room lined with beautifully painted tiles.

There were only a few pieces of time- and war-damaged furniture in the otherwise empty room, but nothing could hide the fact that this had once been a luxurious place, and Lana belatedly realized that they had taken up residence last night in the staff quarters.

Then they passed through a succession of rooms, while Arash seemed to take mental stock. Some were damaged, some merely uninhabited, but all showed the effects of neglect. There were squares everywhere on the walls showing where pictures or other treasures had once hung, and Lana shook her head.

"Did your paintings…?" she started to ask once, and he glanced over at her.

"They were sold to buy arms," he said shortly, and she remembered that tortured night back in London when he had foreseen this tragedy.

She thought suddenly, *If I had comforted him then, instead of just listening, if I had held him and told him I loved him…did I miss my chance then?*

"I'm sorry," she muttered. "This must all have been so beautiful."

He did not answer, merely opened another door and continued on.

Apart from the missing works of art, some of the rooms were largely intact, and as they passed through several of these, she couldn't help saying, "It would be so much better if these rooms were lived in, Arash. This furniture won't take much more neglect."

He nodded. "Yes, I will come home soon."

When you reach my cousin Omar, Arash, I ask that you stay with him for a little, to rest before returning to the Valley of Aram and undertaking the task that awaits you there.…

Arash frowned with the memory. What could Kavi's motive be for wishing him to do this? If he believed

Lana, if she had not requested his escort—what reason could there be for such a demand?

His eyes rested on Lana from time to time as she moved through the home of his ancestors, smiling with pleasure at the sight of a decorated archway, an intricate inlay design on a bedstead or table, floor tiles that his great-great-grandmother's favourite designer had made...why had he been thrust into such proximity with her? Was this incidental to some other purpose that would be revealed only in time?

It was almost inconceivable that Kavian would have feared to give him the details of any mission before he left, and yet...

Make love to me, Arash.

He squeezed his eyes shut against the memories that assaulted him suddenly. Lamplight on creamy flesh, clear dark eyes smiling at him with such open yearning, the heavy weight of her breasts in his hands, the sweet cries of passion and surprise.

He had carried these memories with him across all the battlefields of his bleeding country...and each night dreamed them, as if his soul refreshed itself with a visit to a mountain spring after the daily heartbreak of the wanton destruction of his countrymen's lives.

Arash took a deep breath, his jaw clenched. He would need an iron control to get through the coming days. And last night had made it clear that after such a long period of stress his control was not made of iron.

He opened a door. "This is my mother's dressing room. Some of her clothes may still be here."

He disappeared through the door and she followed him into a corridor lined with drawers and cupboards.

Natural light came through windows high at the far end. He was opening some of the cupboard doors.

"I am not sure what my mother took when she went. Perhaps there is something that you can use."

Lana slowly approached one of the cupboards he had opened. It contained a long rack with clothes covered in white silk bags. The rich scent of spices and musk hovered over everything.

There were several cupboards along the walls, but except for this one, most were empty, or nearly empty. At the end, a wider space filled with mirrors contained a dressing table.

"Where is your mother?" Lana asked after a moment.

"When peace came, she went to live with my sister. She did not like being here alone, where she had been so happy with my father."

"You've been torn by conflicting duties," Lana commented softly.

His eyes met hers as if unwillingly, and he quickly turned away again before she could read the expression in them.

"Choose whatever you find useful," he said.

"Thank you," Lana said softly. She reached into the full cupboard at random and unzipped one of the silk bags. The silk parted to reveal an extremely fine gauze, purple and spangled with diamanté. With a smile she zipped it back up.

If you dressed in something like that, maybe he wouldn't be able to resist you, an inner voice tempted her.

Yes, or maybe I'd just catch my death of cold, she responded firmly.

"Here is something warm, I think." Arash meanwhile had reached into another closet and pulled out a garment bag. He hung it on a nearby hook and with a sweep he slid down the zipper and flipped out the contents.

It was not something warm. It was a soft, shimmering negligee in glowing turquoise. It seemed to have been made with a thousand overlapping feathers in deliberate imitation of a bird's breast, with fluffy feathers also trimming the cuffs and neckline. The front opening parted over a thin gown in silk satin, still faintly wrinkled around the hips from its last wearing.

Perfume wafted from the bag, carrying an erotic potency that said that a woman had worn this outfit....to entice a man.

Lana blinked and shook her head, loosening her neck muscles, to try to clear her thoughts.

"I've never seen anything like that!" she said brightly, to shift her mood. "That's really magic!"

"Yes," he said. "My mother liked to wear beautiful things for my father. He said she was the only woman in the world who could make a man blind to all other women."

They regarded each other in silence, without knowing that time passed.

"Was it an arranged marriage?" Lana asked at last, because surely they were lucky to be so in love if so.

"He saw her one day on horseback, down at the river. My father—his name was Zahir—was a very fine rider, the best among the young men in this valley. My mother and her companions passed him on the road. Her horse bolted suddenly. Zahir and his men gave chase. My father's mount was very swift. He caught up with her and dragged her off her horse and onto his own."

Lana smiled. "Did they fall in love at first sight?"

"She was beautiful, and his blood was up, and with his arms already around her Zahir could not resist. He kissed her."

Hearing the word *kiss* on his lips, she licked her own. "And what happened then?"

"She blushed, because of course such things are not done even today in this valley. She said, 'Is this how an al Khosravi chooses a concubine?'

"My father was furious at the insult. He said, 'It is how he chooses his wife!' He returned her to her friends, learned from his own men who she was, and the next day travelled to her father's house to ask for her in marriage."

"Is all that really true?" she asked, entranced.

Arash smiled. His voice had softened almost seductively as he told the story. "It is the story my father told. My mother sometimes added the information that her horse had only bolted under her instructions."

Lana laughed. Arash started to say something, then stopped abruptly, blinked and stared at her as if she were someone who had shaken him out of sleep, or another reality. He swallowed and turned to the task of repacking the garment.

"I thought it was perhaps a coat," he explained in a low voice, and replaced the garment bag in the closet. "You will come later and make your choice of whatever you need. My mother would wish it."

"A bath!" Lana cried, as her glance fell through an open doorway. "Oh, bliss!" Then she paused, recollecting. "Oh, but I guess it's not working?"

"Neither water nor electricity has been restored," he said.

He stood at the open doorway as she was tempted into his mother's private *hammam* in the semidarkness, touching the beautiful marble and the ornately carved fittings with awed admiration.

He remembered childhood moments here, the room filled with steam, his mother in the tub, laughing at her attendants, or wrapped in a white towel, choosing from the host of scented oils she was offered…how he had loved the perfumes, the hot steamy air, the scent of women.

"What beautiful bottles!" Lana exclaimed.

Some of his mother's soaps and bath oils, dusty with disuse, were still sprinkled around the room, sad testimony to the life of the house that the bombs had destroyed. Lana's eyes were enchanted by the magical glass shapes and the rich turquoise and purple and gold and green oils within.

She picked up one at random, opening it and being transported to another world. These were the scents of a pampered, lovely, and loved woman, a woman with full confidence in her sexuality, who after bathing here had moved to the next room and slipped on a silk slip and a peacock feather robe.…

He remembered his childishly clumsy, excited hands once reaching for a pretty bottle…remembered how the bottle fell to the tiled floor.

A powerful, intoxicating perfume had hit his senses, overwhelming him. He remembered the intensity of that experience, how he had laughed and cried, his body leaping with the thrill of it. He had squatted down to soak his hands in the slick perfume on the tiles, and press them to his face. He had to be pulled away by an attendant because of the broken glass.

They had all been laughing and happy—it was not

his mother's way to shout over a broken bottle. Everyone had been delighted to see his infant ecstasy, the pure sensual joy of the child.

"Ah, what a happy woman your wife will be!" his mother had crooned, but it was many years before he had understood the reference.

Fourteen hundred years ago the Prophet, peace upon his name, had said, *It has been given to me to love perfumes, and women, and the coolness of prayer.* And in the Tribe of Aram it was still said that a boychild who loved perfumes would grow up to be a good husband and a good man, for like the Prophet he would love women and seek his guidance always from Truth....

He had understood the potency of the tribal custom on that long-ago night when Lana had stepped into his arms. That night his senses had been overwhelmed. He had been as wildly intoxicated by her as when the essence of a potent flower had drowned his childish self in an experience richer than any that had gone before....

In another age, another life.

All that was gone now. Only a dozen bottles of scent still littered the low table that had once been crammed to bursting. And one, on the floor, broken in two neat pieces, like his life: the shell remained, but the substance had gone.

He stared at her with a kind of angry intensity, and with a meaningless comment, not knowing how she had offended, Lana nervously replaced the bottle on the glass table.

They moved on. Some doors he passed by without opening, and she guessed that these were his father's and his brother's rooms and that he couldn't bear to see them empty. Not yet.

Soon they opened a door onto daylight. They had come to that part of the house that had been hit directly and was almost demolished, and now she stepped out into the weather, between walls without a roof. It was the section of the house highest up the slope of the valley wall.

Lana stood in the fall of thick wet snowflakes and stared around her at the ruin, a cluster of stone-built rooms without roofs, a pile of tragic rubble, already deep under snow. Window and door frames gaped empty, snow drifted high in the embrasures as if to emphasize the bleakness.

Then, under the pounding of the waterfall, she heard it. A distant sound…

"There is no need to explore here," Arash said.

She clutched his arm. "Arash, what was that?"

Aaaaaa…

"You heard something?" he asked, cocking his head.

A faint, faint cry, gone as soon as she heard it.

"Like someone crying," she whispered.

"What direction?"

She pointed east, towards the waterfall. Arash stepped across the snow-mounded piles of rubble and through a gaping doorway in the thick stone wall that had stood for centuries, and defiantly still stood. She followed him and discovered herself in the broad walled courtyard on the opposite side of the house.

In the centre of the open space was a square building surmounted by the dome she had glimpsed yesterday. Its windows were covered with wooden shutters, its walls piled high with drifted snow.

Aaaa.

Against the sound of the waterfall and the deadening effect of thick snow, it was difficult to get any bearing, but the sound was louder now than before.

"It is possible someone has taken shelter here, not knowing what part of the house is habitable," Arash said calmly. "Let's check the *majlis.*"

The *majlis* was a tribe's place of assembly, set aside by the sheikh for meetings and consultations with his people. In modern democratic countries the name had sometimes passed on to the elected assembly of the central government, but it was still used in its original meaning for these small local meeting houses.

She followed the path he beat through the deep snow of the courtyard towards the domed structure, which seemed largely intact. Her heart was beating uncomfortably. Was it a baby she had heard? If someone had spent the night out here without heat…it would be a miracle to find them alive.

The massive double doors of carved wood opened with surprising ease under Arash's hand, and he drew them wide and stepped through.

Maaa. Maaa.

Lana stepped inside after him. The darkness was relieved by the shafts of light coming through the cracks in the shutters. Nothing relieved the animal odour that hit their nostrils, nor the sudden chorus of bleating that arose in their ears.

"Ya Allah," Arash muttered, more to himself than to her. "Is my father's majlis made a stable?"

"What is it? Sheep?" Lana inquired, blinking at the nervous shuffling shapes that crowded together in the darkest corner.

"Wait," he said. He wheeled around and went out

past her, and a moment later she heard the bang of shutters and muted daylight entered the room. He opened two sets of shutters and returned.

A small flock of sheep crowded into one corner of the room on the beautiful black-and-white-tiled floor, where straw had been laid to give them a bed. A few chickens and a rooster wandered around pecking the straw at random. A mule by a pail of meal stood patiently chewing, watching them over his shoulder.

"Oh, thank God they survived!" she exclaimed.

"Look," said Arash.

Farthest into the corner, facing the newcomers four-square, a ewe stood protectively over two tiny, perfect newborn lambs who suckled and pulled with crazy intensity, their tails waggling ferociously.

"Aww," chanted Lana, and then laughed with delight. "Oh, how brave of her, to lamb in the middle of a blizzard!"

"It is early for the valley. Lambing usually doesn't start for another two weeks."

"Are they warm enough?" she asked. The combined animal body heat had provided its own warming system, but the two lambs were so tiny.

"Lambs survive worse than this," Arash said. "But they will have a better chance if they are kept warm for the next few days."

She followed the direction of his nod. In the opposite corner there was a high iron stove; behind it was stacked coal and wood.

"I was hoping we could look after them in the kitchen!"

Arash flicked her an amused glance. "Try telling their mother that."

He crossed to the stove and, lifting off the plates on

top, looked down inside, then opened the door at the front and crouched down to begin manipulating the lever that shook down the ashes. She saw a glow of red.

''Well, we know that Sulayman or someone was here only yesterday,'' he said. He carefully picked up a few tiny bits of wood and began to feed them to the embers.

Lana crossed the room to help him, searching for dried leaves and twigs among the logs and passing them to Arash. After a few minutes the fire began to crackle and spit.

Plenty of fodder had been spread for the animals by someone who had clearly not expected to return for several days. But they freshened the fodder and the straw bedding, and took the oak buckets standing by the door and emerged again into the snowy day.

They worked together mostly in silence, and every time he seemed to anticipate her moves, or she anticipated his need, feeling stabbed her heart.

We could have worked together to rebuild all this, she told herself, as she watched Arash striding through the snow. *He would have accepted Dad's money if he loved me, and we could have...*

If only. There was no use crying over it.

Then, suddenly, a voice was murmuring, *Suppose I told him I loved him, asked him to marry me? Would he marry me for the sake of rebuilding his heritage? Would I marry a man who only wanted my money?*

But he didn't have to marry her. She had offered him help freely, no strings, and he had rejected it.

Out of pride, whispered the voice. *But if you were married, that would give him an excuse for accepting.*

Buy a man with my father's money? her other self demanded angrily. *No thanks.*

You'll never get him any other way.

She shook her head, shutting the voices out.

Arash crossed to where a narrow stream tumbled over a terraced wall in a tiny waterfall, and filled the buckets under it. Lana stood watching, then followed him back inside the building.

Standing in the doorway behind him while he topped up the water in the troughs, she saw that as he straightened his gaze was drawn as if irresistibly to the centre of the wall directly opposite the big entrance doors.

There was a large round shadow in the exact centre of the wall. She could not see his expression, but she saw how his back stiffened and he deliberately turned away from the sight.

"What was there, Arash?" she asked impulsively, before she could stop herself.

Arash turned to her blankly, as if surfacing from a dream. "Pardon?"

She indicated the wall. "What used to hang there?"

"The Shield of Aram," he said. "It hung in that spot for two hundred and fifty years."

His voice was without expression, but somehow she knew this had been the most precious treasure, was the worst loss of all.

"It was sold?" she asked quietly.

"Sold? No, it is impossible for the al Khosravi to sell Aram's Shield. It bestows sovereignty and right guidance upon us. Once, long ago, it was stolen, but the thief returned it. Now it has disappeared again. Who knows where it has gone?"

Eight

By unspoken agreement, when they returned to the kitchen, Lana began to make preparations for lunch while Arash filled the paraffin heaters and brought one into the kitchen and lighted it. The other he kept in the next room, where after a few minutes she heard the sounds of shifting furniture.

They had found supplies in various pantries and storerooms. There was enough food to keep them going; the amounts were small but there was more variety than she had feared they would find: olive oil, onions, apples and potatoes, dried lentils, chickpeas, apricots and milk, wheat flour and rice, and some bottles of home-preserved tomatoes. There were herbs and garlic hanging from the ceiling in one room, along with several joints of meat.

Gazing up at these, Arash had murmured, "The protection of the *majlis* comes at a price."

"And if you'll get me down one of those, please," she had responded dryly, "I'll try to find some way to cook it for your dinner."

But for now she was concentrated on making their midday meal, and the sound of Arash's activities next door became a companionable accompaniment to her own work. It was pleasant to feel that they were working together, on different tasks, towards their common good.

Back in London, when she had been falling for Arash and hoping he was falling for her, when she believed he was Kavi's bodyguard and had no inkling of his wealthy and aristcratic background, she had sometimes dreamed of a life like this, far away from the world she knew.

She had imagined them together maybe on a small farm, raising children and animals in a happy mix.

Lana had never wanted a marriage like that of her parents, where a close family life was sacrificed to the creation of wealth. Her father had been away most of the time, her mother taking sole responsibility for the home and family, at the end of ten years finding herself rolling in money but with little in common with her husband.

No, she hadn't wanted that with Arash. She had hoped for a life of sharing—the hard work and the joy, the pain and the pleasure....

But she wasn't forgetting that it was only because of her father's long hours of hard work that she was here now. If her father had been an ordinary man with ordinary goals, she might never have decided to go abroad to university, never have met Arash, would probably hardly have heard of Parvan or the Barakat Emirates.

And even if she had, she would have had no money to spend on the country's rebirth.

She had set some beans to soak earlier, and now she peeled, chopped and lightly fried onions and some canned tomatoes. She tossed them into the soup pot, added water and herbs and spices and set the result on the brazier to cook—a thick country soup—and removed the pail of water she had set to heat there.

Then, slipping her small bag of toiletries into her waistband, she picked up the pail of warm water and a lamp, slipped under the rug in the doorway and into the room beyond.

There she stopped in amazement at what she saw. "A stove!" she cried. "A real, honest-to-God *cookstove!*"

Revealed because Arash had removed a lot of the massed furniture and boxes, it stood in one corner—a marvel in black iron and chrome, dated and in need of a good polish, but otherwise looking serviceable.

"Imported from England for my grandmother. She thought it would make life easier for the cooks," Arash said.

"Does it work?"

"The pipe used to go out there, where the damage is," Arash told her, pointing to the missing section of roof and wall. "It will not be usable until I find some substitute for the missing lengths of pipe."

Lana looked around. There was also a large clay oven of the kind that was typical in the countryside. So this was the original kitchen. "Is that one in working order?"

"No problems there," Arash said. "What time will you want it hot?"

"Probably about three, is that okay?"

She indicated the pail of warm water. "If you don't mind, I'll go up to your mother's bathroom to wash. I guess the drains will be working, even though the water isn't."

He nodded. "I will carry the heater up for you." He suited the action to the word, bending to pick up the paraffin heater and leading the way along the corridor and up the stairs.

He was so caring, so protective, and she wished with all her heart that it was herself that he loved. Or that he loved no one, and she could hope, with time, to make him love her....

Did he know whether the woman he loved was still single? She wished she dared to ask. Suppose his love had grown tired of waiting and wondering and had taken second best? Maybe Arash was in a hurry to return home to prevent exactly that.

Maybe he was already too late. Was that the fear that haunted him, that was shadowing his eyes more and more darkly since they had come here?

Would Arash consider marrying her, Lana, if his true love were lost to him?

She was brought up short, seeing where her thoughts had inevitably led her. *It wouldn't work,* she lectured herself. To marry someone you loved more than he loved you was one thing. When he loved someone else, how could such a marriage possibly bring anything but heartache? A man who didn't even start out loving his wife would treat her badly, make her life hell.

Not Arash, her heart whispered. He was so careful of anyone for whom he was responsible—she had noticed that about him long ago. She was sure he was a man who would always be caring and protective of his wife, even if he didn't actually love her.

Except for that moment last night, she reminded herself ruthlessly. He hadn't been kind then. But then, what had that been, except an admission that he could still find her sexually attractive, even when there was nothing else between them?

If she married him, it would be important that he at least find her sexually attractive....

Absently she watched his tall, too-lean body moving with unconscious masculine grace ahead of her. Something in the very shape of him seemed to affect her mental function, her heart.

Stop thinking like this!

Ahead of her, Arash opened the door to his mother's bathroom and went in to set the heater down in the middle of the floor. Lana, following, set down her pail and slid the little lamp onto the nearest flat surface.

"You brought a light?" he asked.

She reached into her pocket and held up the flint, and Arash took it from her hand and lit the lamp for her. As he restored the glass chimney a comforting glow warmed the room. For a moment they stood looking at each other.

"Don't forget to make use of my mother's clothes."

"Are you sure she won't mind?"

"She will mind only if she learns that you did not use whatever you needed."

"Thank you."

He moved to the door, turned and looked at her.

"Will you stir the soup?" Lana asked, feeling the sweetness of ordinary things. "I won't be very long."

"The soup," he said slowly, as if he were thinking of something else. He moved his head and his gaze shifted. "Yes, I will stir the soup."

The bathroom and the dressing room were both well-stocked with mirrors, so when Arash said his mother was beautiful that was the truth. Well, she would have known that anyway, just looking at Arash.

Lana was one of those rare creatures—a woman unconscious of her own beauty. Perhaps because she had been raised without an adoring father to reinforce her sense of her own value, but also because since well before puberty she had been what other women considered fat. And although she herself had never worried about her weight, nor felt it to be a problem—she liked food far too much for that—the constant pity of her weight-obsessed fellow students couldn't help making a mark.

Of course men told her she was beautiful—even more beautiful because she didn't know it—but she had learned early to distrust that. Deep-set chocolate eyes with dark eyebrows, a straight, small nose, wide full lips and broad cheekbones carried all the ingredients of beauty, but she did not see them that way. Lana knew she was attractive, but if Arash had high standards of beauty…

She stood straight in the chill air, briefly examining her own naked body in the mirrors. She had lost a lot of weight since coming to Parvan, and she had cut her thick, once waving hair short, so that it curled around her head. Life was a lot easier this way, but she wasn't really used to seeing herself like this yet. Ever since puberty she had worn her hair long, had been well-rounded.

Now she was as slim as a boy. The rounded flesh had gone from her upper arms, her thighs, her abdomen, her bottom, and her body still felt strange to her. Her once-heavy breasts were smaller now.

She wondered if Arash would find this body attractive. Would he find pleasure, as he had once before, in stroking her neck, her thighs, her breasts? The thought of his touch, of touching him in love, abruptly made Lana go weak.

I do not believe you have forgotten.

She had forgotten. She had forced herself to forget. But now she remembered, and if he touched her again the way he had last night…Lana closed her eyes. She would be so helpless. If he stroked her, if he kissed her…

"Okay, this is what they call cabin fever," Lana muttered sternly, opening her eyes again. "Down to business."

She lifted a pretty smoked-glass bottle and tipped a few drops of turquoise oil into her bathwater.

"You found something to wear," Arash said, as they sat down to their lunch. Soup, and some stove-top biscuits, and apples for dessert.

She was wearing a flowing kaftan in a woven mix of deep indigo and purple wool. It was thick and warm as well as being feminine. And she knew the dark purply blue was good with her skin, enhanced the gold highlights in her hair.

What she didn't notice was that it also emphasized the shadows around her eyes, giving her skin a look of delicate porcelain, so that the past months of hard work seemed to have demanded too much of her.

Making her look as if she needed protection.

"You have been working too hard," Arash said, ladling soup into a bowl for her. He also had changed his clothes, from jeans into traditional Parvan trousers and cotton knitted knee-high moccasins, a long shirt, a dark vest. He was a mountain man now, no one could have mistaken him for anything else.

Lana stared at him. "All I've done is make lunch and a few preparations for dinner!" she exclaimed. "You're the one who's been throwing furniture around!"

"I do not mean here and now. I mean, you are less healthy than when you came to Parvan. I am glad Alinor makes you take this rest."

Accepting the bowl from his hands, she blinked at him in surprise. It was the nearest thing to praise Arash had ever offered her.

"I thought you resented my interference," she observed mildly.

He picked up his own empty bowl and paused to gaze at her. "Resented your interference, how?" he asked in astonishment. "In Parvan?"

Lana picked up her spoon and began to stir the steaming soup. She nodded wordlessly, not quite looking at him.

"That would be insane, if it were true. Because of you what would have taken years has been accomplished in months! How could any Parvani resent such interference?"

"You think I'm a poor little rich girl, playing at being Lady Bountiful, though," she murmured, staring at her soup with the fixity of a child hoping to find the letters of her name.

Arash finished filling his own bowl and set it down on the table with a clunk. "No," he said. "No, Lana, I do not think this of you."

The soup was nicely flavoured, the beans just a little undercooked. But they crunched satisfyingly this way. Taking another spoonful, she glanced up at his face.

There was a strange, indescribable mix of emotions on his face.

"Then why will you never accept help from me?" she asked reasonably, lifting an inquiring hand. "The way I see it, you'd rather let this place subside in a heap than take money from my father—or even any of the charity funds—to restore it. And that would be a pity, because it was beautiful and it could be again."

She held the full sleeve of the robe with one hand as she reached for one of the stove-top biscuits she had made, and carefully concentrated on breaking it in two. Its moist white centre steamed. Then she was forced to look at him again.

His dark eyes searched her face for a deeply unnerving moment when she could not read his expression at all, and just as it seemed something had to happen to break the tension, something inside him withdrew, as if by an effort of will. His gaze fell to his own bowl and he sipped some soup.

"It is not possible."

His tone was one she knew well. Remote, coming from behind a closed door. She knew from experience that the door was locked.

But she pushed against it anyway. "Why is it not possible?"

"But it does not mean that I remain blind to what you do for the country."

"But why can't you accept…"

"I cannot discuss this with you, Lana."

"I don't see why not. There's only the two of us here. Who is there to be offended?"

She thought she had made him angry, by the way he applied himself to his soup. He did not reply. Arash seemed always able to retreat into a world where he was alone.

They ate their soup in silence, while Lana wrestled with her feelings. She wanted to tell him, to say, *Look, I love you, I've just realized I'm crazy in love with you and have been right from the beginning, are you sure you don't love me?*

But she had done that once already.

Her words hadn't been quite so blatant, but she had been clear enough. Dumb with misery because he had left her without a word, she had written to him, in Parvan, as Kaljuki troops massed along the border and the world did nothing....

By then she had learned from Alinor who he was: not Arash Khosravi, a bodyguard, but Arash al Khosravi, Cup Companion to the Crown Prince and younger son of a titled sheikh.

Then she had understood, or thought she did: that was the explanation for everything that had happened. Why he had first seemed attracted, and then not, and then, when she threw herself at him, why he had been unable to resist. That was why he had said he could offer her nothing.

Because he could marry only with his father's approval, and his father would not approve of his interest in a foreign nobody....

In the letter she wrote that she was sorry not to have said goodbye, said she would miss him, said she hoped that peace was still possible, that she looked forward to meeting him again...and then she had written sadly that she wished he had been an ordinary man, without a title, because then, perhaps, they could have been more to each other....

As close as she could get to a declaration without

actually begging. In her dreams, Arash would write back, would confess the truth of his position, tell her why their love was impossible. In her dreams she then told him the truth of who *she* was, and asked him if this fact would change his father's mind.... She had had high hopes, because however aristocratic the family, she did not believe that the sheikh would object to such a marriage for his younger son. Arash was not his heir, after all.

So she had hoped. Arash replied with only the briefest of notes, thanking her for her concern. He had signed his real name, but there had been no explanation. There was nothing at all to give her hope. Not even the most tangential reference to the fact that he had made unbelievably wild and passionate love to her the night before leaving, that he had cried aloud, had wept and been shaken as he took his pleasure from her....

Nothing.

By then the Kaljuk army had invaded, the airports were closed to all but military traffic. Lana did not write again. She accepted what she should have understood from the biginning: he was never interested in her. He had made love to her because she had agreed to totally uncommitted sex and he was a man with normally functioning hormones.

There was nothing at all to regret except her own blind, self-centred stupidity.

And she was not going to go through the humiliation again of offering herself to the man who didn't want her.

When they had finished, Arash cleared their bowls from the table while Lana spooned coffee and sugar into a little pot and set it on the brazier, then set out a pretty hand-painted bowl with a few winter apples. They were wrinkled but still very edible, and with every sign of enjoyment Arash caught one up in one hand and bit into it with strong white teeth. The perfume of the fruit was suddenly deliciously sharp on the air.

"Are these from your own orchards?" she asked, taking one herself.

"I hope so," he said. "If they are not it will mean our trees are not producing."

Lana bit into the apple, feeling the juice spurt up into her mouth. The flavour was strong, richer than anything she could have bought at home, and under the skin the flesh was still firm and very white.

In spite of everything, she felt suddenly at peace with him. She thought, *I couldn't remain angry with him for long, no matter what he had done.*

"Is Aram an ancestor of yours?" she asked.

He was silent a moment, and over his face flicked a look that tore at her heart.

"Aram," he said, tasting the name. He nodded thoughtfully. "A long-distant ancestor, about whom we have many legends. He was the chief of this valley, a renowned warrior, a man who had attained deep mystical power."

"Is the shield really so old?"

"The shield, no. The stone—the central ruby of the shield, that was Aram's."

Lana smiled, biting into her apple again, and settling down on her cushions. "So it was originally Aram's Ruby?"

"That is what we call it. Aram's Ruby is carved with symbols that are said to draw power and seal it in the stone. The ruby was mined in this valley—in ancient times there were ruby mines here, and it was the finest and largest ruby to come out of those mines.

"Aram himself carved it, for only he had the knowledge that was required. Whether he wore it, or used it as a seal, is not known. So the stone was passed down from ancient times through this family. More than five hundred years ago, my direct ancestor had the ruby set into the centre of a ceremonial shield of gold, silver and copper, inscribed in such a way as to renew the power captured in the stone.

"The people of this valley believe—have believed for hundreds of years—that their good luck, happiness and prosperity comes from this shield, for as long as it is in the possession of their sheikh, he will be rightly guided. If a leader is rightly guided, no evil can befall the people."

He paused, thinking, seeming not to notice that he had let silence fall. She saw that he was contemplating an uncertain future.

After a moment, he roused himself. "The shield can bring such fortune only on its rightful owners, the al Khosravi sheikhs. It cannot be sold, and anyone who stole it would bring evil on his own head."

"Oh!" Lana had completely forgotten the apple in her hand. "You mean, there's a curse on it?"

He smiled and shook his head. "Not a curse. If an ignorant man sticks his finger into an electric socket, it is not a curse that kills him, but his own ignorance of what power is there, and how it must be used."

A little shiver of uncertainty threaded her fascination in the story, for his voice was the voice of a man explaining not arcane secrets, but simple fact.

"But, Arash…do you believe this?"

He gazed thoughtfully at her. "Lana, there is a hydroelectric dam at the head of this valley, bombed by the Kaljuks, which your father's money is at this moment helping to restore. Why?"

She was startled by the sudden change of subject. "Well, because electric power is so…it's so important to people's standard of living. What do you mean, exactly?"

"Do you believe in the electric power of this dam?"

"Believe? No—I mean, yes, but I don't have to *believe* in it, it's just there."

Arash smiled, then went on with his story.

"The shield, Aram's Shield, was displayed to the tribesmen at every meeting of the *majlis,* and when the present *majlis* was built—the building that now houses chickens and lambs and a mule—the shield was given a permanent home there.

"That was two hundred and fifty years ago. And over time, the *majlis* came to be called *Dar-i Khoshbakti,* the Gate of Good Fortune, because it was through its means that good fortune entered the valley."

When he paused, Lana remembered her apple and took another bite. She wanted to ask *Who stole it?* But the storytellers of Parvan did not need prompting. Storytelling was an art that all, from the simplest to the most sophisticated of Parvan's citizens, practised and understood.

"So the shield hung undisturbed through many years, and at every meeting of a *majlis* the men of the valley who had gathered to talk to their sheikh could see the proof that the sheikh's guidance could be trusted, and he could be given their loyalty.

"But word of the ancient stone and its strange properties spread. Men came from abroad, scholars and academics and seekers and charlatans and many others, asking to see Aram's Shield. At first, all such requests were refused. It was not until my great-grandfather's time that the first Westerner saw the shield.

"And one day in 1917 a servant tremblingly approached my great-grandfather with the dreadful news. Aram's Ruby had disappeared. The shield hung where it had always hung, but the stone had been prised from its place and the shield had no longer a centre."

Arash paused.

"What did he do?" Lana gasped, for, although Arash's voice was calm, she could almost feel the anger of the sheikh resonating down through the years.

"The day before, three men had visited the *Dar-i Khoshbakti* and viewed the shield. A Frenchman and two Englishmen. It was impossible to say whether they had worked together, or if one had done the deed alone. My great-grandfather's servants had not troubled to notice who had been left alone with the shield, or in what order the men entered and left the *majlis*— to them it was unimaginable that such a theft could occur."

On the brazier, the coffee suddenly boiled up in the little open pot, breaking the spell, and Lana snatched it from the heat. She had set two tiny cups, and she filled them with the thick, frothing liquid.

Arash stirred extra sugar into his while she asked, "What did he do?"

He smiled a smile that made her glad she was not the thief. She thought, *The old sheikh was probably terrifying. What a fool the man was to cross him.* "My great-grandfather of course did nothing. He shrugged his shoulders and wondered aloud that foreigners were such fools as to toy with their fate in such a way.''

Lana opened her eyes at him. "Is that really what he did? Didn't he even try to find out who had stolen it?''

Arash shook his head.

"He summoned all the men of the valley at once to the *majlis* to show them the despoiled shield. He reminded them that the stone would bring evil luck on the thief, whoever he might be. He assured them that the Ruby would soon be back in his possession, not through force, but through its voluntary return by the thief, who would not be able to bear the weight of evil luck that would now befall him.

"And that is exactly what happened.''

Lana's mouth opened. "Really?''

"Within three weeks the stone was returned to my father by a guide who had been paid a huge sum to deliver it, with a letter from one of the men begging forgiveness.''

"Is that all it said?'' she wailed.

"It said that nothing but evil had befallen him since stealing the jewel and he hoped to forestall more by sending it back to its rightful owner.''

She gaped at him, amazed. "Arash, that's really strange!'' she said. "Is it true?''

He smiled at her with a tenderness in his eyes that melted her heart with wishing. "It is true. The letter was kept—it may even still be here. Certainly I saw it as a child. It was written in very stilted, broken Parvani that made me laugh.''

"Do you know what really happened?''

"No,'' he said. "All that is known is that the ruby was returned by a very frightened man.''

Lana suddenly remembered the tragic sequel. "Do you think that will happen this time?" she asked.

Then she wished she hadn't spoken, for all the light went out of Arash's eyes as he was reminded of his loss. He shook his head.

"I know nothing of how it disappeared. Perhaps it was moved from the *majlis* and destroyed in the bombing. Perhaps it was stolen and the thief died without leaving a trace of where he hid it.

"I do not even know when it disappeared. I had not spoken to my father for many months before he died, nor my brother," he said. "We fought on different fronts. And there have been many strangers in the valley, during the war and after."

She didn't know what to say. "Is it...it must be extremely valuable," she murmured at last.

"It is one of the world's largest known rubies," Arash said flatly. "The engraving is unique. It is of inestimable value, both to collectors and to jewel merchants."

"I'm sorry," she murmured—because that made recovery of the jewel so much more unlikely. She had learned something of the antiques trade through her father's museum, and she knew enough to understand that if the shield had fallen into the hands of a private collector it might never see the light of day again. But at least in such a case it might be preserved intact.

The situation was a thousand times worse if an unscrupulous trader were to prise the ruby from the centre of the shield and recut it. It would still be valuable cut into two or more smaller stones, but the historical value of such a unique piece would be destroyed.

In that scenario, the shield would probably survive. It would still be valuable as a collector's item without the stone, but would be worth little if melted down. No one would trouble to destroy the masterpiece.

"But Arash, don't you think if a stranger—if anyone had gone out of the valley with the shield someone would have noticed and remembered? Have you asked people if they saw anything?"

"No one knows yet of our loss. Only Kavi, Alinor, and now you. Even Sulayman believes that my father removed the shield for safekeeping. When they learn the truth…" He shook his head and looked at her.

She saw desolation in his eyes. "How will I tell my father's people that, in addition to their other griefs, the source of their good fortune and right guidance has been lost forever?"

Nine

"**A**rash," she whispered helplessly, putting a hand on his arm in an automatic desire to offer comfort. She looked into his face. "Will it mean so much to them?"

He gripped her hand and lifted it away, as though he couldn't take having her touch him. But then, having captured it, he didn't let go. Instead he turned it palm up, within the clasp of his own hand, and gazed at it as if the answer to his problem might lie there.

"Even now they say that the Tribe of Aram escaped the worst of the Kaljuk bombing because of the protection of the shield."

"Do you have to tell them the truth?"

His thumb stroked absently across her palm in a gesture of intimacy that shook her. It was as if they had a lifetime's history of turning to each other for comfort. As if, for this moment, he had forgotten the actual,

ordinary circumstances of their relationship in favour
of some deeper truth of what was between them.

Her heart leapt with the first hope she had felt since
those distant days when everything had been possible.

"The meetings of the *majlis* must be reinstated as
soon as I return to the valley. They will learn at the
first meeting. There is no way to tell them. There is no
way not to tell them."

She offered hesitatingly, "I suppose you wouldn't
lie to the people about when it disappeared?"

He lifted his gaze to meet hers with the searching
look that was so much his hallmark. She had seen him
look at others like that, but not usually herself, not
since she had come to Parvan. It had been as if he had
no interest in the inner Lana Holding, not even as much
as he invested in strangers at fund-raising parties.

But now his gaze pierced her, and she lost her breath
because of the way her heart leapt with the desire to
reveal herself to him.

"What do you mean?"

"If they attribute their relative good fortune in the
war to the shield and you tell them it was already gone
before intensive bombing began, doesn't it follow that
their luck is not attached exclusively to Aram's
Shield?"

The rich colour of his thoughtful eyes was something she would have been happy to drown in. She
thought absently, *One day I'll have a home with a
stained glass window that is just the colour of Arash's
eyes....*

"Start my life as their leader with a lie for their own
good," he pondered aloud. "Would it be the first evidence that the al Khosravi are no longer rightly
guided?"

He shook his head, and smiled at her.

"They are men and women, not children. This would be to treat them as less than my own equals. I am the leader of my father's people because they have chosen it, because it is best for men to unite under a leader, not because they must accept me. Such a lie would violate the contract that my ancestors forged with the people."

Suddenly she saw how deeply honourable he was, with an honesty that went right through the bone.

"I'm sorry," she murmured. "You're right."

"There is no reason to apologize for offering me advice, Lana," Arash said with that same thoughtful frown. "Sometimes advice that is not taken is the method by which we find the right road."

"If you want my opinion," she said before she could stop herself, "the Tribe of Aram is safe in your hands with or without Aram's Shield, and give them a few weeks or months and they'll realize that."

He smiled at her, but the worried frown was still there, behind his eyes.

A thought was taking shape in the back of her mind.

"Arash," she murmured tentatively.

His dark gaze met hers inquiringly.

"You know my father is endowing a museum. What if—what if he put it out on the grapevine that he was willing to buy Aram's Shield, no questions asked? He could offer a massive sum, you know, and that might tempt the thief out of hiding."

He stared at her. "And what then, Lana?"

"Well, don't you see—if he was contacted by whoever has it, and tipped you off, you could have it seized and impounded as stolen property."

He was silent, considering. "And your father would

risk this? Such a person might be very vengeful, Lana, if he discovered your father was behind it.''

He was right. And her own connection to Parvan was so well known the thief would guess immediately that it was a deliberate trick. She dropped her eyes.

''Or he could just buy it,'' she said tonelessly, knowing what was coming.

He looked at her. ''The museum would fall down around his ears if your father tried to keep the shield there.''

''I didn't mean to keep.''

''You suggest he should buy it and give it to me?''

''Why not?'' She couldn't look at him, knowing in advance what his answer would be.

''Lana, Aram's Shield is worth perhaps many millions of dollars to a collector. Why should your fath—''

''On the open market.''

''What?'' He blinked at the interruption.

''On the open market, with bidding, I agree the sky's the limit with something like the shield. But what your thief has to face is that he can never sell it on the open market. It's stolen property, and no way can he ever hope to disguise that fact, from now till doomsday.

''So he has to take the money and run, Arash, don't you see? Whoever has stolen it, unless they stole it to order for a private customer, he has to take whatever he can get. He can't be hoping for more than a million or so.'' She paused, thinking.

''Maybe not even that. My father told me—''

She broke off because he was laughing. ''Only a million?'' he asked, with ruthless irony, as the closeness she had felt was washed away. ''Is that all? Well, then I will sell a few of the sheep that my father has left to me, and pay your father back!''

"A million dollars is pocket change to my father, Arash," she pointed out, with a rueful inward smile for what her father's reaction would be to hearing that.

She saw suddenly that she had angered him. "I know it!" he said. "He can buy and sell an impoverished sheikh, why not? What shall I give him in return, then, Lana?" He stared at her, as if seeking his answer from her face, and she was caught and held by his gaze.

"What have I to offer except myself?" He lifted his hand to her head, and she felt his fingers close ruthlessly in her hair. "Shall I marry his daughter so that his grandson will inherit an ancient title? What else is there to tempt him to do this thing for me?"

"Stop, Arash," she muttered uncomfortably.

"And you, Lana, you who can hardly stand to be polite to me—will you consent to being part of such an exchange? Your son would be a sheikh. Is that worth the sacrifice of your happiness?"

Her own fury blew up, consuming her with burning heat.

"How dare you!" she bit out. "Where do you get off suggesting that my father would demand any return for what up to now has been pure generosity? How can you say such a thing about him? Or me?

"If I wanted to marry someone for his bloody *title,* Arash, I sure as hell don't have to choose you! You have an *obsession* about being bought and sold! What's your problem? All you have to do if someone makes an offer, you know, is say no!"

She stared at him. "Or maybe that's what you're afraid of, Arash! Maybe you're afraid of yourself!

Maybe you're afraid you *are* for sale, and you couldn't say no! What's the matter, is the shield too great a temptation? You might be seriously tempted to marry a woman you can't stand if it was to get your shield back?''

"I am sorry, Lana," he began, but she overrode him, jumping to her feet.

"Is that why you turned down my offers of help, is that why you'd rather be in constant pain every second of the day than go and have surgery paid for by me? Because it might be a disguised attempt to buy you?

"Well, set your heart at rest! I won't be putting in any bids in your direction. If I want to buy a man, there are lots of ancient titles in the world, Arash! Why should I stop at the sheikh of a tribe in a country no one's ever heard of? I could have an English duke's son for the amount of money my father can afford to throw around. I could probably have a European prince. You get to wear a tiara with a title like that, you know!''

He struggled to his feet. "I have apologized already, Lana. You must not insult my name."

"No, no, naturally I must not!" she agreed with bitter mockery. Of course her anger was given impetus by the thoughts she had been entertaining over the past day, and of course she was in no state to admit that to herself. She waved her hands in the air.

"It's open season on *Holding*, it's all right to suggest that my father's generosity is just a cover for the purchase of human beings, but *al Khosravi*, now, there's a name that..."

He grabbed her wrist in a hold that made her gasp. "Stop this!" he commanded. She could see that he was keeping his own temper in check only with difficulty.

"Let go of me!" she cried, twisting her wrist, but he held her firm. "Let go!" Her other hand came up to push against his chest, and suddenly, unbelievably, they were fighting.

"Stop it, Lana, stop it!" he cried, catching her other wrist, and then for a moment they were frozen, her hands in the air, caught in his grip, their bodies close, staring into each other's eyes.

"Ya Allah!" Arash cried helplessly, his jaw clenching. And then slowly, inch by inch, as if drawn by some powerful, slow-working magnet, he drew her arms around his neck, let go of her wrists to slide his arms around her, and wrapped her body tight against his. For one long second they gazed into each other's soul.

"I warned you," he said. "But you would have it so."

And then his mouth pressed hers in a ruthless, demanding kiss.

Her body was suddenly at melting point, and she moaned and clung to him, igniting him so that they burned together.

He held her head and tormented her with his kiss, a deep, hungry kiss that sucked her lips and nipped her tongue, that burned and melted her mouth, until she was whimpering with need. She cried his name under the pressure of his lips, fuelling his need, making him hungrier for the taste of her desire.

His mouth was a drug to her. The more he gave her, the more she needed. When his hands clenched helplessly in her hair and, drawing her head back, he tore away from one kiss to press another against her throat, she moaned aloud both pleasure and loss.

Then, one hand cupping her head, the other against

her lower back, he pressed her body against his, bending her back till she lost all sense of balance, making her feel his hard arousal and the assault of his tongue at once, and the world went black.

He pushed her onto the cushions and followed her down, his hands and his eyes burning her. He reached over her for more cushions, tucking them in around her, under her head, under her hips, so that she could be in no doubt of his ultimate intent.

He held her with such firmness, such strength, such possessive determination—and feeling the surge of passion in his blood that both thrilled and frightened her, she wondered dimly, *Is this what it means, to be safe in the lions' den?*

He was both danger and safety to her, and her blood trumpeted the knowledge in her temples, her heart, her whole being.

He did not smile as he looked at her. "Lana," he said, then bent to touch his lips to her eyelids, her temple, and trail kisses down the curve of her cheek to her ear, her neck, her throat, where the neckline of the kaftan left bare the pulse of her heart.

The kaftan buttoned down the front. He undid the buttons, one by one, his hand firm with purpose, his eyes fierce with need. Underneath, her soft breasts were covered only by the thinnest silk, and he pressed his lips against her flesh through the frail covering, so that heat rushed through her.

She lost track of time. What happened was measured by her heart only, beating, melting, sighing. Once only had she experienced this tenderness, only once before had her heart opened so trustingly to the being of another.

The air was cool on her skin when he drew off the

robe, but it only added to the passionate heat, the shivering desire that coursed through her.

Then she was above him, her body still encased in the silk garment she had taken from his mother's closet, her breasts on his chest, and she smiled into his eyes while his hand stroked her shoulder and arm, her face and hair.

"Do you give yourself to me like this, without conditions?" he asked, and she only smiled and helplessly shook her head.

"What conditions do you want me to make?"

"None," he said roughly. He gazed up into her face, seeking her response.

She only looked at him.

With a whispered oath his hands came up to encircle her head, and he drew her irresistibly down till, as if after a long age of need, their lips met in a kiss.

How much she had ached for his touch, through all the time of waiting and fearing to hear that he was dead, and afterwards, knowing that he disliked her, not knowing her own feelings…a flood of sweet yearning burst through her like an exploding sun, melting, burning, sweeping away everything in its path, as his lips, his mouth, his tongue pressed and devoured hers now with a hunger that bruised her.

"Oh, Arash," she breathed, when his hands and mouth released her at last. "Oh, Arash, your mouth!"

The violet eyes darkened as he gazed at her. He kissed her again, wildly, as if the taste of her lips made him drunk.

She undressed him, with passionate patience unbuttoning his shirt and pressing first her palm, then her lips against the heat of his chest, waiting with hungry eyes and melting being as he pulled off the moccassins, the heavy cotton trousers called *shalwar*...

Then she opened her lips on a soundless gasp, closed her eyes and opened them again, taking in the sight of his virile power...and the brutal scar that marked his leg from knee to groin.

He watched her from eyes that had gone black. Her gaze met his.

"How beautiful you are, Arash," she murmured and, his eyes leaping with the impact of her words, his hands slid sensuously up her thighs, drawing the silk high to expose her body to his need. Then he pulled her naked hips over his, parting her thighs until she was kneeling astride him, fitted himself to her, and drew her down onto his wild, desperate flesh.

Ten

She lay in his arms and wanted to weep for pure joy. He had pulled a quilt over their heated bodies, and now he held her tighter than she had ever been held, his hands firm with possession. Her heart was wide open.

She lay against him in the clasp of his naked arms, his hands on her at hip and shoulder. She rubbed the flat of her palm lazily against his chest.

She counted his heartbeats, and listened to the ever-present rush of the waterfall, and thought they were the same. Everything was a manifestation of love.

And she asked, "Arash, do you love me?"

He stiffened. His hand convulsively squeezed her arm in warning. "Lana, do not ask this question."

Her heart, so open, began to shrivel with the hurt.

"Why not?"

"I have nothing to offer you. You know it." He

paused, but she could not say a word. "You yourself want nothing from me."

"You're sure of that."

"This," he admitted, stroking her arm from shoulder to elbow. "Of course, pleasure you wanted and you accepted. Let this be enough for both of us. Do not ask about my heart."

She lifted herself to look down into his face. It was tight with anguish.

She said, "I have a right to know one thing."

"Do you?" he asked, his voice resigned.

"When we were making love just now, Arash—were you thinking of me, or of her?"

He closed his eyes briefly and turned his face away. When he opened his eyes again he was not looking at her.

"Her?"

"The woman you love. The one who's waiting till you put your life in order. Were you making love to me, or to her?"

His chest rose and fell in a deep sigh. His mouth twisted. "You, Lana. I made love to you." His eyes moved to find hers again, and she saw the torment in them and pressed her lips together against a gasp.

"I'm sorry!" she whispered, not knowing why she said it.

"I am sorry, too. A man has no right to be so weak and still to call himself a man."

Tears burned her eyes, and to hide them from him she abruptly sat up.

"Are you—attracted to me against your will?"

"You know that it is so," he said flatly. "Why will you speak of it?"

He wouldn't be the first man who was sexually attracted to someone because he thought her easy, while reserving his love for someone pure. *The virgin-whore fantasy,* she saw with sudden clarity, *and I am the whore.*

A snort of bitter laughter escaped her. Cast as the whore by the man who had been her only lover, who had made love to her all of twice in her life!

"I speak of it because we should get it straight, shouldn't we? I don't want you blaming me, Arash! If you make love to me, that's your choice, not because I seduced you, okay? I could just as easily—"

"I do not blame you. The fault is my own."

She shivered and reached for the purple robe, which, she saw now, almost matched his eyes. No doubt that was why she had chosen it. But it made no difference, and she pulled the robe over herself. She found strength in being covered.

She rubbed her fingers through her scalp, briskly ruffling her hair, and turned and found his eyes upon her. Eyes that, in spite of his best intentions, no doubt, were still packed with desire.

It was like being kicked just under the ribs. Lana took a deep breath.

"So what do you want to do now?" she asked.

"Do?"

"We've agreed that we have the hots for each other, Arash," she pointed out brutally. "We're holed up here together and now we've taken the lid off something you wish we hadn't.

"What are we going to do about that? Are we going to spend our energy fighting it, are you going to be loyal to your dream girl—or are we going to take the next couple of days as a moment out of time?"

His eyes squeezed shut in a grimace of torment that

shocked her. "You drive me mad!" he said hoarsely. His hands closed painfully on her flesh.

"What vision is this that you conjure up for me? That we should love each other while we are here, freely, without thinking of the future, and when we leave, we leave it behind?"

She opened her mouth and closed it again. It would be a huge mistake. She knew that if she let him love her now he would bind her heart to his so that she would never be free of him again. After one night of his lovemaking, she had been left unable to let another man touch her.

She had tried, she had wished desperately to wipe his memory from her skin, out of her heart, with another man's touch. In the years between then and now other men had kissed her in passion. Each time she had hoped that this was the cure. Each time she had erupted with awful, uncontrollable rejection, pushing them away as if... No amount of apology could make up for what she had done, though she had tried. *I'm sorry, I thought I was over him....* After a while she had stopped trying.

If he made love to her again, if she gave in to the passion in her heart and in his eyes—she would be marked forever. When would she be able to settle into an ordinary life?

For him it would be a few days out of time. For her, it would be all of her life compacted into a few short hours. Hours of tormented, incomplete bliss. Her body sated, her heart still seeking. Or worse still, pretending. Hoping to change him, to see him fall in love with her.

But she swallowed and looked at him and knew she could not turn her back on her only happiness, even if it was destined to be only a crumb.

And she said, "Why not?"

Then, when the die was cast, she gasped with fear. But before she could take back the dangerous, foolish words, he jackknifed up, his hands encircled her head, and he drew her down and down, to drown in his ruthless, ravenous kiss.

His body grew hard against her thigh, as hard and hungry as if it had never tasted her flesh.

He was the lover she had always dreamed of. He was everything she ever wanted. He was passionate and tender, wild and firm, strong, loving, beautiful.

For two days and nights they made love, with such intensity and devotion she sometimes imagined that the world could only end on the third day. As if something inside them knew that the earth's life span was unbearably short, and they had to live all of life's passion in those two days, as if their frail human bodies carried the whole burden of expressing the joy of creation in the teeth of extinction.

Desire was a constant. He would catch her wrist as she lifted an apple, and the apple would fall from her suddenly helpless grasp, rolling away somewhere as her tongue tasted the sweetness of him instead of the fruit. It struck them anytime, everywhere. Their eyes could not meet without sparking the need.

She had not known so much pleasure was possible from the human body. And she made such discoveries over and over in the tiny moment of time that was allotted to her for joy....

He became to her the physical embodiment of her pleasure. Everything he did, all that he was, had the power to move her. He was a magnet, and she was a highly charged piece of metal. If he left the room while she sat in it she had to restrain herself from following him.

The lightest touch, a glance from crushed-violet eyes, even the movement of his hand in lamplight melted her. Made her yearn and ache for his kiss, his body, the wild explosion of delight that their bodies together created....

It was delicious, it was sweet, it was painful in its intensity. It was cruel in its lies, the voice in her head that whispered that he must love her, that such meeting and melting could not be possible unless he did....

It was like being drunk on the wildest champagne she had ever tasted. It was like flight on her own wings, and knowing she was too close to the sun. It was like dancing for him alone, wild, abandoned, freer than she had ever hoped to be...and knowing that the music would stop, soon, brutally.

"It's so hot!" she murmured on the second night, when they had awakened to need deep in the night and a wild burst of sensual excitement had made her sweat.

"The storm is over. Come," he commanded, standing up and drawing her up after him. She was drunk with sensuality; every cell seemed swollen with the constant shift between need and satisfaction. She followed him mutely, shivering a little as her feet touched cold tiles....

He opened the door to the outside and led her out into a black, snow-covered world. She stopped on the threshhold, blinking. The snow had stopped, the moon was high and bright in a silken sky, the world silent, magical, holding its breath as it waited for them...even the waterfall's music was muted in the darkness.

They were both naked, and she looked at him in

sensation-drugged shock as he lay down on his back in a bed of snow and pulled her down after.

"Arash!" she cried.

He pulled her thighs apart over him, and his hand found her centre with practised ease and she instantly melted into the hot spiral of pleasure that coursed through her. He fitted her to his body, and drove into her, pulling her hips ruthlessly down.

Her knees deep in cool powdery snow, she fell into the hungry rhythm, in spite of having been sated a thousand times, and began to pant as his body in her hard and demanding, pushed against the floodgates in her…it was a dangerous touch, giving him a connection not only to the deepest wells of pleasure in her but also to her heart.

Then, as the pattern built towards explosion, he picked up a handful of snow and thrust it against their flesh where their two bodies met.

The icy shock against the high heat they had created was a system overload. Cold and heat rushed and clashed in their bodies, creating a pattern of sensation that made her cry out and laugh and gasp and moan.

Trembling with inexpressible pleasure, Lana's head fell back and she cried her amazement to the sky from an open throat, like a songbird who has just discovered that morning has come again.

"Arash!" she cried, as his heat burned up into her and he pulled her down into his embrace and kissed the word on her lips.

Eleven

Under a wide, clear sky, two snowshoe-clad figures moved across the white valley towards the caravan route and the high pass. The sun that crept up over the mountain peaks was already warm, and all along the valley animals, their bells tinkling in the pure air, stepped gingerly out of their winter pens and sniffed at the deep white blanket that covered the valley.

Progress on snowshoes was difficult on the slope, and Lana had never used them before. But Arash went slowly, and she followed behind, trying to copy his step, his use of balance.

They had left money and a note on the table. It was customary in the mountains to leave some acknowlegement of the involuntary generosity of your hosts in such a situation, and payment if you were able. Arash of course was not a guest in his own home, but the money would allow Suhail and Sulayman to replenish their supplies.

They had renewed the animals' feed and water, and left the door of the *majlis* open.

A host of little tasks that reminded them that the real world would soon return. Only once, as they reached the crest of the ridge, did Lana allow herself to look back at the valley. The peace of it filled her heart, and she breathed deeply. She had spent a few days and nights of delirious pleasure in his valley, his home, his bed, his arms…and that would have to last her.

Under the thick fall of snow there were few visible reminders of the war, and she looked at the valley and imagined that this was almost how it had always looked in winter.

"Does it look the same?" she asked.

He bent to her lips, not having caught her words. "Pardon?"

"Is this how it used to look before the war? In winter, I mean."

He straightened and looked at the scene, considering. "It is not so different, I suppose."

She pointed to where a thousand blackened skeletons reached up through the snow, much more obvious now against the snow than they had been on the evening they had arrived. "What was there?"

"An apricot orchard," he said. "A bomb hit it in a dry summer."

"Whose is it?"

If things had been different, if there had been no war to take him away from her, might he have brought her here one day, to look at the valley not so different from what she now saw? If he had stayed in London, might the powerful physical bond have grown into something stronger, more durable?

"My family's."

"Yours, now?"

He glanced at her. "Mine, while I live. Mine to care for and pass on."

She said, "Arash, I'd…" She swallowed nervously, frightened of rejection. "I'd like to… would you let me replant it? Just that? We could bring in the saplings as soon as the snow melts…I hate it when trees…"

His lips tightened behind his curling beard. "Ah, did you enjoy it so much? What a compliment to me, Lana! Think what I can tell my sons in some future moment—this apricot orchard I earned in the bed of a rich American woman! How they will—"

"Shut up!" she cried, her voice ringing. "Shut up! What right do you have to say that?"

His face closed with anger at himself. "None. I have no right to say such a thing to you. Forgive me."

"Why did you talk to me like that?" she demanded, her voice breaking as she fought the quick tears. "Why did you spoil it?"

"In order to spoil it for myself. I am a man divided against himself," he said, his jaw clenched. "You know it. It is the road to madness."

He turned away up the path. "Come," he said.

The towers and domes of an *Arabian Nights* palace hovered shimmering above the capital of Central Barakat.

Lana unconsciously braked, her mouth opening on a slow gasp. "Is that it?" she breathed.

They had crossed the border into the Barakat Emirates and the Koh-i Noor mountains the first day. In the afternoon the road had begun to descend, and they entered the last long tunnel that the engineers had blasted through a mountain, emerging much lower down, in the foothills of the Koh-i Noor.

That night they had stayed in a village, where they were given an impromptu feast by the local chieftain, attended by all his neighbours for miles around.

This morning they had been escorted on their way along the sparsely travelled desert highway by a swashbuckling guard of honour in four jeeps. After an hour the guards had fired a farewell volley into the air and then, with grins, cheers and salutes, had peeled off in a wide sweep to return the way they had come.

"I suppose they've been doing that for centuries, only on horses," Lana marvelled.

"You suppose right. It's a very old custom, escorting your guests through hostile territory. Not quite as necessary as it used to be."

"Maybe he's a sheikh of the old school," she suggested, and he smiled.

"We are all sheikhs of the old school. There's no new school yet."

And even a simple sentence like that could melt her, she discovered—because she knew that the old code of behaviour, along with hospitality, generosity, and noble warfare, included giving sexual pleasure to your wife.

She flicked him a glance and was rewarded with the hard clasp of his strong, finely sculpted hand on her wrist as she held the wheel.

"Lana, it is finished now," he said. "We left it behind in the valley."

Last night in the village, of course, she had slept in

the unmarried women's quarters, in a tiny room with a high window through which she could see the moon as she lay awake aching for him.

"I know," she said.

Now the palace shimmered in the heat like a mirage, seeming to float in the air above the ground, as if her own mind had conjured it out of a fairy tale.

Arash nodded. "Omar's palace. It was the winter palace in the days of the old king. The court only spent certain months there—the rest of the time they were at the seaside or in the mountains."

"I can relate to that." Lana grinned. "It's hot enough already, isn't it?"

"Glad we've finally arrived?"

Not exactly. "I'm certainly looking forward to a shower."

The truck windows were open to the burning desert heat. Now and then, without warning, dust devils blasted sand into her face. She wore sunglasses to protect her eyes, and a large silk scarf around her head, because, however it ranked as a religious duty, covering your hair was a practical necessity in the desert.

Arash nodded and wiped a hand over his forehead. His face was streaked with sweat and dirt, and she supposed hers was the same. His hair and beard were dusted with sand.

She had a sudden vision of him as a middle-aged man, still strong and virile, his face lined with maturity, his hair greying, and her heart trembled with the desire to be with him then....

"A shower, yes," he said.

Suddenly there was a cloud of dust in the distance,

and they heard the sound of firing. Along the highway towards them, and off road, too, a phalanx of a dozen jeeps was bearing down on them.

Lana's heart sank. "Oh, God!" she cried. "Who are they?"

Arash said simultaneously, "Ah, we've been sighted! Omar must have sentries posted."

She had still to get used to the traditions of welcome. Hospitality, like generosity, was a high art in Parvan and Barakat alike.

She laughed. "For a moment there, I was regretting the sheikh's departed escort. I thought maybe we were being taken hostage!"

"What, so close to the palace? I think Omar would have something to say about that!"

In a swirl of dust, the jeeps surrounded them, guns firing on all sides. A few mintues later, they were escorted into Prince Omar's palace.

Omar's wife, Princess Jana, led her to a magnificent suite of rooms that was to be hers while she stayed in the fairy-tale palace. Two women servants were already unpacking Lana's bags.

"This is Salimah, who speaks English," Jana said. "She will take good care of you. Salimah, this is Lana Holding. And Fatima will draw you a bath."

The introductions performed, she led Lana out onto a broad terrace, cool, shaded, that faced on an internal courtyard where a beautiful fountain played at each end of a long still pool surrounded with bright flowers and rich greenery. Colonnades of delicately wrought arches surrounded the pool on four sides to provide shade. The sun entered through delicate latticework and fell in entrancing patterns.

"This is enchanting," Lana said.

There were drinks already waiting, on a low table between two comfortable chairs. Princess Jana waved aside a third servant as the two women sank into their seats.

Lana, still in dusty boots and jeans, was feeling very grubby beside Jana's stylishly cool white shirt and pants and gold sandals, but she certainly needed a drink before anything else. She chose the mixed fruit juice, and while they chatted Jana poured and handed her a tall glass of peach-coloured liquid.

It was at the state wedding of all three princes of the Barakat Emirates that Jana and Lana and Alinor had discovered they already knew each other. Although they had attended different colleges of the University of London, they had belonged to the same swim club. It had been a casual acquaintance—they had never even known each others' last names.

It was strange how much of a bond it seemed, now, so far from home.

"Alinor and I were terrified when that blizzard blew up," Jana was telling her. "We were on pins and needles. Thank God you made it to the valley! But Omar said right from the start that you were safe with Arash. He said it was just my own guilt making me worry so much."

"Why should you feel guilty?" Lana asked.

Jana floundered a little. "Oh, well, just because…you know how it is! I invited you, after all!"

"Yes, but—" Lana began, but her brain refused to concentrate on mental puzzles now, and she let it go. "Oh, isn't this wonderful! So beautiful—look at the way the sunlight falls through that lattice, it's just magical." She stretched luxuriously in the sun-dappled shade and drank the sweet mixture of peach and lime and other fruits she couldn't distinguish.

It was delicious. Lana sighed with satisfaction, listening to the fountain play. "I suppose Arash's place was something like this, before the bomb," she remarked.

Jana sipped her own drink. Hurry seemed a million miles away.

"Is it very bad, the damage?"

Lana described what she had seen, the remnants of pools and orchards and arches, the beautiful tile work all broken, and then fell silent.

"I suppose now that you've seen it, you'll find some funding for him?"

Everything was too close to the surface for Lana to pass it off. She looked at Jana, no longer trying to disguise her hurt, from herself or anyone else.

"I've been offering money to Arash for ages. He won't take a cent from me."

Jana's mouth was open in a small O of surprise.

"Really?" She was mystified. "But how ludicrous! And all this time we thought—but *why?*"

Lana shrugged. "You tell me," she said, and the tears were suddenly very close to the surface.

"He won't even—not even the apricot orchard! He practically bit my head off—I mean, hell, Jana, what's a few damned *trees!* And I *know* his knee could be helped, it's a piece of shrapnel or something, but will he let me pay for the trip or the surgery? Will he, hell!"

She began to sniff, and set down her glass to hide her face in her hands.

"Oh, I'm going to cry! All this time...nothing! He

even helps raise the funds, for God's sake! I told him once if he only would accept the money that his targets donate after he's talked to them... but he just says, *Yes, use it on the valley.*"

"The valley but not his family estate?" Jana queried thoughtfully.

She nodded vigorously. "That damned dam the Kaljuks were so careful to—God, they were monsters! If you could see the careful way they targetted irrigation systems that have been there for centuries!

"All of that kind of stuff in the Valley of Aram— I'm allowed to fund that. They accepted their quota of the spring seed, and of course the teams went in and did mine clearance.... And we got a small textile factory going in one of the villages—traditional Aram textiles are really popular on the West Coast and in France, for some weird reason."

A sob rose in her throat as the pain that she had never allowed herself to feel came surging up.

"But that's all he lets me do. When it comes to..."

"Lana, he must be in love with you." The quiet voice cut through the misery in her brain like a whip.

"What?" Lana gasped, her breath trembling on whispered sobs.

"What other explanation is there?"

"Why is *that* an explanation? If he loved me he'd be able to take help from me!"

"If he lived in California, maybe. Arash is from the mountains. He's a Durrani *and* an al Khosravi, you know. Both fierce mountain tribes."

Lana gazed at her friend, torn between crazy hope and disbelief.

"Omar's a Durrani, too, so I know," Jana went on.

"The very fact that Arash loved you would make it impossible for him to accept your help. Up in the Koh-i Shir range a man's a man, and he looks after his woman."

A man does not marry until he has something to offer a woman.

"But he loves someone else. He told me so."

Jana stared. "Did he? When?"

A servant helpfully appeared with some neatly folded tissues on a tray, and with a grateful smile, Lana took a couple, and blew her nose.

"Boy, no staff problems here, I see!" she joked, as she wiped her nose. "He told me a couple of days ago. When we were up there. I think she's a girl from the valley. He said he wasn't going to marry her because it would take him years to rebuild and it would be a waste of her youth and beauty—as if she'd care about that if she loves him!"

Jana shook her head sadly. "Well, then I don't know what to say. Funny how we thought—" She broke off, and at Lana's inquiring murmur, merely shook her head. "You don't suppose he's lying to protect himself?"

"From what?"

Jana looked at her. "From you. If you had no money and needed him, instead of him needing your money—you might have a better chance, Lana."

"There was a time in England that I thought—maybe his father wouldn't want him to marry a foreigner. I wondered if maybe that held him back."

Jana smiled. "All I can say is, it never seemed to cross Omar's mind.

"Now, you must be dying for your bath, and here's

Fatima to say it's ready. *Shokran jazilan, Fatima,*'' she added to the servant, who nodded and disappeared again. "Fatima doesn't speak English. Most of the servants don't, but you won't need it with her, she's very capable."

Jana got to her feet.

"Omar and I are both scheduled to attend a banquet tonight in Barakat al Barakat, and then we're in talks all day tomorrow. So I'm afraid you and Arash will be on your own here for the next couple of days."

Lana blinked up at her. "What?"

"I'm so sorry, but there wasn't anything we could do about it. Of course, I'd planned on your being here a few days ago, and we would have invited you to go with us, but I'm not going to ask you to sit through a boring banquet tonight when you've only just arrived.

"I've left instructions for your meals to be served here on the terrace. I hope you'll make yourselves at home. There's a swimming pool, horses, cars, whatever you need—Arash knows the palace well."

Jana bent over her and kissed her cheeks. "I am sorry, I'd love to be able to sit and talk all night, but it'll have to wait. The helicopter has to leave in half an hour if we're going to be on time, and I've got to get into formal dress. But you'll be fine. Just ask Arash if you want anything."

Lana stood silently appreciative as Fatima rubbed her all over with perfumed soap, like a child. The touch of her firm hands relaxed the muscles that were stiff from long hours in the truck and sore from Arash's passionate lovemaking.

Afterwards she moved down the steps into the bath

and felt her body's grateful melting into the warm clear water.

She was trying not to think. Trying not to use Jana's words as the centrepiece of the puzzle that was Arash's behaviour. Trying not to hope...

He loved a woman but had never told her so. She remembered how his eyes had seared her as he told her that...was it possible?

It made sense of everything, and especially the wild passion of the past few days. If he loved her but could not marry her because he had "nothing to offer"— then the days of their lovemaking meant...

Lana closed her eyes and tried to banish the bright hope that flooded her to the roots of her being.

Thirty minutes later, totally refreshed, she stepped into the bedroom.

"Oh, how lovely!"

Salimah blushed with pleasure at the praise. "My mistress instructed me to offer you the use of her wardrobe, Khanum Lana. Seeing that you brought so little with you, I have chosen some for your approval tonight."

Several fabulous outfits were laid out, and Lana admired each in turn, though she knew from the first glance which she would wear. Salimah smiled in delight as she chose it.

"It is very beautiful, because it just reveals the skin," she confided, lifting the diaphanous black trousers that were crusted with gold embroidery around the ankle and handing them carefully to Lana. "Of course one wears no underwear—that would spoil the effect," she confided with a smile.

So Lana slipped on the flowing black harem pants and tied them at her waist and, putting her arms into the intricately gold-embroidered black jacket, watched in the mirror as Salimah buttoned it. Salimah was right—the gauzy fabric seemed opaque until her skin came in contact with it, and then it was revealed as diaphanous.

She used only the lightest of makeup, except around her eyes, which Salimah expertly kohled for her, and then dusted her cheeks and eyes with a gold powder that was all but invisible.

Then the maidservant placed a circlet of delicate gold leaf coins around her forehead, and draped the outfit's sparkling cobweb scarf around her hair.

Simple gold thong sandals and a few bangles on her arms completed the outfit. Lana stared at the vision of herself in the mirror. She would be staking everything on this night. What if he thought her a fool?

Well, why shouldn't he? She was a fool. A fool for love.

Twelve

The table was laid by the fountain at one end of the terrace. She moved around to it under the beautiful stone colonnades, through the soft twilight, feeling as though she walked the path that a thousand women had walked before her, and with the same goal in mind.

The perfume of night flowers came softly on the desert wind, and a single star glinted down on her.

Venus. Goddess of Love. Oh, shine on me tonight.

He was there already, standing by the fountain, watching as her shape slipped from column to column, coming nearer to him.

He had said that it was over when they left the valley, but tonight he knew that it was not over yet. He had not been able to resist her in a snow-filled valley, a bombed ruin—how could he resist her now, when the heat of the desert night surrounded them, and she was dressed like the paintings of his ancestors' concubines, when the perfume of a thousand blossoms overwhelmed them, and her own sweet scent called up his blood?

She stopped at a distance, nervous, as though sensing his desire even that far. How had he been such a fool as to let his resolve weaken? To believe that there was such a thing as a moment out of time? He would pay the price of his blindness all the rest of his life, the memory of her clouding all that he did.

"Lana," he murmured. Her name was true for him as for all his countrymen. She had melted the heart of anguish, had softened the misery that life had created for him…but at what price? The pain of loving her he would never forget.

The gauzy, glittering scarf half-hid her smiling, trembling mouth from him, so that he saw instead the trepidation that filled her eyes.

He frowned.

"Why do you fear me?" he asked hoarsely. "How have I hurt you?"

Had his passion taken him too far? Sometimes he could not remember afterwards, so drowned was he in the taste of her.…

She shook her head. "I don't fear you, Arash," she whispered.

She was lying, he could feel it. He knew her. He understood her with a directness that did not need words, now. If she feared him…

He would have more control in future. He would not allow himself to be so lost in her.…

A moment out of time, he reminded himself. *There is no future. Tonight, yes, because anything else is impossible. But it will be the last.*

A servant noiselessly appeared to light and place

candles in clouded globes around the terrace, and they moved to sit at the table.

Tiny jewels all over her gauzy stole flickered in the candlelight with every movement, surrounding her head with a thousand fireflies. The fine gold medallions that rested on her forehead tinkled like fairy bells, creating a symphony in his ears. He had dreamed of her like this, in a glow of light and music, smiling at him.

"You are very beautiful in the costume of the East," he said softly, watching how the candlelight burnished the pale skin behind the silky black that covered and revealed her arm, her shoulder, her breast, as she moved. She was like a sculpted dancing girl in the bottom of a silver winecup, revealed and then hidden by the movement of the wine...like wine, she was intoxicating to the senses.

"Thank you."

He was a prince from the *Arabian Nights* himself, in loose cream-coloured Parvan trousers and a flowing, wide-sleeved shirt jacket that was open over his powerful bare chest. He was barefoot, his strong feet caressing the ground with full, deep connection. Just with that connection had he made love to her, and she felt the recognition of it in her deepest self....

Her eyelids drooped in seductive yearning as she looked at him, and his flesh stirred with the thought of her desire. She would not look at him like this if he had not pleased her. His hand clenched involuntarily around the crystal goblet, and he focussed his eyes and forced it to relax.

"Jana says the servants don't speak English."

"One or two, perhaps, but not those who serve us tonight. What is it you wish for?"

She smiled and shook her head.

"It's a beautiful night," she said softly.

More stars were appearing as darkness fell. Nearby an insect buzzed loudly as it sucked the sweetness from a night flower.

That was what she was in the glimmering black—a night flower. He thought how he had sucked the perfume from her, and a drunken madness flooded him, telling him to lift her in his arms now and carry her to his bed. If it was to be their last night, he must give her something to remember forever.

A beautiful night. *Beautiful,* he thought, *but cruel, for it has shown me my own weakness, how unequal I am to what fate has brought on me.* He thought of all that was in his heart, all that he could never say to her, even on a night like this....

"It is a beautiful night," he agreed tonelessly.

She looked at him from her dark eyes and smiled at him.

"I've never been in a place quite like this. Jana says you know the palace well."

"I visited often as a child, with my mother. During the war, I came here to—" He paused. "I came again."

"When you were wounded?" she suggested.

He inclined his head.

The servant placed food in front of them. Something luxuriously succulent, only to be expected from Omar's kitchens. The contrast to the practical, plain food they had eaten in the past hardworking months, and especially the past few days, was almost too shocking for their palates. They ate for a few minutes in silent, sensual enjoyment.

"It's been a long time since I tasted anything as delicious as this," Lana murmured. *Except for you.*

"Omar always has excellent chefs." He marvelled at his own ability to speak of nothing when the truth pressed up in his throat, urging him to confess, this once, all that he felt.

"Was it in Barakat that you had the surgery on your leg?" she asked.

He nodded. "Omar's company of Companions was with us that day. It was Omar's quick response that... He flew me himself in a helicopter. If I had had to take my chance with the field doctors..."

He did not finish. She gazed blindly at him, wondering how close she had come to hearing the news she had dreaded to hear. She licked her lips.

"I'm glad he was there," she whispered.

The waiter removed their plates and rolled a silent trolley near the table. It was a kind of portable grill, and he began to prepare some exotic flaming dish. They watched in silence as his skilled hands danced within the flames to produce the magic.

"Your hands are like that," she murmured, half-unconsciously.

He stared at her, the flames marking his face with leaping light and shadow. His jaw clenched. He could not speak.

"Dancing in flame," she explained softly. "When you touch me, it's fire."

Their eyes met and held. Blood leapt in his body. He closed his eyes and silently breathed.

After a moment the delicious odour of cooking arose over the table, and two plates of delicately sliced sizzling meat, redolent of sensual spices, were placed in front of them.

Lana inhaled the wonderful smells. It was as if the meal had been designed with seduction in mind, an assault on the senses—sight, smell, touch, taste.

"Do they eat like this all the time?" she asked. Even with all his money, her father didn't pay this much attention to food on a regular basis.

When they had finished serving, the waiters bowed and withdrew against the wall at a distance, where they stood like sentries.

"It is a cultural bias. Recollect how few sensual delights there are in the desert," Arash said. He looked at her. "We make the most of those we have."

She dropped her eyes to her plate. Oh, he did that, all right.

"In the desert, maybe," she managed to say in a normal voice. "Right here in this palace I've seen plenty, though. I don't know when I've seen so many flowers in one place."

"If you come to the Valley of Aram later in the spring, you will see flowers in great profusion," he began, and then broke off.

"But I won't be coming to the Valley of Aram later in the spring, will I?"

His jaw clenched. He made no reply.

"Tell me about the flowers in the valley," she begged. "Because I will never see them."

He swallowed.

"Please," she whispered.

He told her then, lovingly, because he described flowers to a flower. He told her a story from his valley, of the nightingale's love of the rose. How it yearned and pleaded from a distance, how it never won the rose.

He told her of his love thus secretly, knowing that her heart understood even if her ears did not.

Flowers, the shape of arches, the desert winds. Softly they discussed such things. But every word was a cloak for some other meaning. Every movement of his hand, her mouth, as they ate the tempting food, was a message of another kind. Every nod of her head made faint, sweet music.

Every sense was engaged on one theme: love.

Above them the stars became infinite in number, and the moon rose.

At last some rich honeyed cream, of unbelievable sweet delicacy, was served. The sweetness was painful to him, like his love, for it spoke of another world. A world where love and perfection were possible.

Lana slipped the spoon between her lips as he watched. He thought how he had taught her to taste his body between those lips, how willingly she had responded to his tutelage....

"So, it's over, our moment out of time?" she breathed then, as if reading his thoughts.

"Yes," he replied.

Then, because he could not resist: "Tonight—if you, too, wish it, we will have tonight. But it must be the last time."

She nodded, licking her lips. Just so had she licked her lips after...

"Is it because I don't please you, Arash?"

His hand gripped the stem of the gold-traced crystal goblet as his heart kicked a wild protest.

"It is not because you don't please me," he said levelly. "You know it."

"I pleased you?"

"I say that you know it! Why do you persist in this?"

"Because I would like to hear you say it. I think I have the right to hear it, don't I, if I've earned it?"

"What else have I been saying, here in the night? Did not you understand? You understood!" His jaw clenched, but she only gazed at him, silently pitiless.

"You pleased me," he said, and could have laughed—or wept—at how pale the statement was compared to the shimmering truth.

"My body is a source of pleasure to you?"

He stared at her with burning, crushed-violet eyes. "Your body is my torment and my delight," he said.

He closed his eyes against the flood that threatened him. So much feeling. How long had he kept it locked in? Would there ever be another woman who would respond to him as she did?

A wave of passion swept her at his words, and she swallowed and clung desperately to her purpose. She took another bite of the delicious dessert, and the creamy sensation on her tongue was as rich as the taste.

"I wonder," she said dreamily, "if you were a sheikh of old, whether you would have added me to your harem."

He moved jerkily, pushing his upper body back out of the candlelight. His eyes black, the deep purple lost in the shadows, he gazed at her.

"What is it you want, Lana?"

"Do you think you would have?"

"No," he said.

She gasped, and his eyes burned into her.

"The sheikhs of old did not add women such as you to their harems, Lana," he said bitterly. "Even they were not so lucky. Do not tempt me with such foolishness.''

Her mouth opened on a silent, slow, indrawn breath. ''Why not a woman such as me? How am I different?''

He did not answer.

Her cries in the night as his body moved in her, as his tongue caressed her, his hands gripping her of their own accord, saying that she was his. Would there ever be another woman like her?

''How am I different, Arash? Why am I good enough for three days in the mountains but not as a permanent resident of the harem?''

''Stop it. You are a rich woman, as rich as a queen! How should I have hoped to bring you to my harem?''

''Rich?'' She looked at him. ''Are you talking about money?''

He made no reply.

She took a deep, calming breath.

''What has my father's money got to do with anything?''

''I have nothing to offer you but sexual pleasure. Take that, one last time, and then let us forget.''

''After tonight, never again?''

His jaw clenched, his eyes closed, she saw his fingers unwrap one by one from the bowl of his goblet, as though taking all his concentration, as the servant silently appeared to refill it with clear liquid that splashed and sparkled in the candlelight.

''Aren't you forgetting something?'' she said.

He opened his eyes to watch her.

''I think it's a tradition amongst your ancestors, isn't it, when a woman has pleased you, to grant her some boon?''

His eyes flashed purple fire.

"If there is anything I have that you could wish for, I give it to you."

"You grant me whatever I ask without waiting to hear what it is?"

His head went up, and she saw the shadow of a long line of proud sheikhs behind his shoulder, men whose pride had expressed itself in generosity. She had heard stories of such leaders, and now she saw how deeply he shared their blood.

"Ask your boon," commanded Sheikh Arash Durrani ibn Zahir al Khosravi.

A chasm as wide as her whole life opened at her feet. On this moment's courage rested all her future. She thought of her father, the risk he had taken, borrowing ten thousand dollars and staking his future on his own talents. *My blood is the blood of risk takers,* she told herself, and picked up the dice of life.

She took a deep, trembling breath, and tossed.

"I ask you to marry me."

He sat unmoving, a statue, as though to contain his reaction to her words he had turned instantly to stone.

She waited to hear him say whether she had won or lost the toss.

"Why do you say this to me?" he demanded, when he could speak.

"Do you grant it?"

"I can neither grant you such a thing, nor refuse the gift I promised. Lana, choose something else."

"Why can't you grant it?"

"Why?" he repeated furiously. Then, as if goaded, he began to recite,

*"tora doost daram
wa chizi nadaram*

joz sipar-i Aram,
ke tora nadadam."

"What does that mean?"

"I love you, and there is nothing in my possession,
save for the Shield of Aram, that I do not give to you,"
he translated. "It is what my ancestors have tradition-
ally said to their wives on the wedding day. At such a
moment, in the Valley of Aram, a woman asks for her
dowry. What could you ask of me, Lana, what could
I give you, that you do not already have?"

She looked at him gravely. "The apricot orchard."

She saw the impact of her words only in the sparkling liquid in the crystal goblet that his hand en-
wrapped where it sat on the table. It trembled in the
candlelight.

"The apricot orchard is burnt," he whispered.
"What can you want it for?"

"To replant it."

"That is no dowry for a woman like you," he said
harshly.

"My father has money, Arash, it's true. So naturally
it isn't material possessions I seek for a dowry," Lana
said.

"You have a sense of purpose, a history, you have
something to build and nurture and pass on to future
generations. The apricot orchard is a symbol of all
these things, and it is also a symbol of the opportunity
to do things that matter in the world.

"That is what I ask as my dowry."

She lifted her head proudly and looked at him, a
woman negotiating her own marriage contract.

"On such terms, Arash Durrani ibn Zahir al Khosravi, will you marry me?"

Thirteen

"And for this you wish to marry me? For a sense of history and the chance to do good?" He shook his head as if to clear it. "It is as you once said to me—you may find this anywhere. Marry a duke's son and save his heritage from death duties and the tax man."

"It is not for that that I want to marry you," she said, shaking her head. "I want to marry you because I love you. In keeping with your tradition, however, you have asked me to name my price. I—"

He leaned forward into the light so that the violet flames leapt to burn her. "You love me?" he burst out harshly, as if he could not bear to hear it. "Recollect that until three days ago you hated me!"

"I love you," she repeated, her heart swamped by the release of saying what she had kept hidden so long. "I have never hated you, though it is true you have hurt me. I've loved you almost from the first time we met, and everything I know of you tells me that I couldn't find a better man if I hunted for the next hundred years.''

''What has occurred between us is no basis for thinking you love me. It is sexual madness, Lana—''

''Is it? I wouldn't know.''

His eyes narrowed and he pierced her with a look that searched her soul. ''What?''

Tears burned her eyes as she smilingly blinked at him. ''I have nothing to compare it to.''

Arash got to his feet so abruptly his chair fell over. A servant moved on little cat feet, but was waved away.

''You drive a man mad.''

She gazed up at him, trembling with every emotion she knew, and some she'd never felt before. He stood over her and grasped her wrist.

''You have finished?''

It was a command. She dropped the tiny silver spoon, nodding mutely.

''Come!''

Her heart was leaping in her breast like a wild salmon struggling upriver to spawn. As Arash, waving away yet another servant, pulled back her chair, she stood.

In the furious, concentrated silence of forced control, still holding her wrist, he led her slowly along the colonnaded terrace and down the far side of the sweet pool that lay quietly reflecting the moonlight and stars. Flowers rustled as they passed, stirred by insects or the wind, and, with nature's generous abandon, released their perfumes on the night air.

Halfway along, directly opposite her own suite of

rooms, he opened a door and drew her inside. A beautifully furnished sitting room, like her own, that had been softly lighted by the hands of invisible servants…he led her through to the bedroom, closed the door and turned to her.

"Now," he said grimly. "Tell me the truth."

"There's only ever been you, Arash," she said. "So I'm a bit out of my de—"

"You were a virgin?" His voice was almost an animal cry.

She blinked slowly, gazing at him. "You didn't guess?"

He stared at her, seeing it all again, that moment when he had entered her and her throat had opened on a cry of pleasure, surprise…pain? But he himself had been so lost.

"How should I have guessed it? You offered yourself to me freely, you said nothing that a virgin might say in such a moment.…"

"No," she agreed. "As I recall I said, *Make love to me, Arash.* Is that what I said? Is that what you remember?"

He closed his eyes.

"It is what you said." They were silent. He opened his eyes.

"Why do you tell me this now?"

"Well, because—" She took a deep breath, looking into the distance. "Because if tonight is our last night I guess it'll be a long time before I—"

She broke off.

"Do you tell me no other man has touched you since that night?" he demanded hoarsely.

"Touch is a funny word. They could touch me, they

could even kiss me. But there's always that moment, isn't there, when something changes? When it's not a kiss or a touch, when it's the first step to making love…''

She blinked, and he saw the spangle of tears on her lashes.

''I never got past that moment with anyone. No matter how firmly I told myself that this would be it, that I was getting you out of my system—I never made it.''

His eyes were narrowed with incredulity—and something else—as he stared at her. ''From then until now, how many years—no one? Why?''

''Because I loved you. And I suppose because—because you were fighting a war. Someone would kiss me, and I'd think, *I can't do this when Arash might be hungry and thirsty, or wounded, or having to kill someone.…*''

She squeezed her eyes shut. ''I couldn't do it, not when you were on a battlefield somewhere…but the real truth was—not when it wasn't you.''

With a wordless cry, he wrapped her in his arms, and his mouth found hers, hungry, desperate. She swayed as passion swept her being, mind, body, self.

He tore his lips from hers, bent and lifted her up high in his arms, and carried her towards the bed. In the softly lighted room, his eyes devoured her. He laid her on the bed and sat beside her.

Her scarf glittered on the floor behind them, where it had fallen, a symbol of the unhappiness that had shrouded her. That, too, was floating away.

Gently he lifted the golden circlet from her brow, set it down.

''Lana,'' he breathed. ''I must learn to be less of a fool.''

He stretched his long body beside hers, lying above her on one elbow, and tenderly stroked her cheek, her ear.

The look in his eyes gave her courage.

"Arash, who is the woman you said you loved?"

"You know who she is."

Her stomach swooped. She closed her eyes, wondering if anyone had ever fainted from happiness, then opened them again to drown in the purple depths.

"It is you, Lana. It is you whom I love and have been afraid to love."

"Oh, Arash," she breathed, and his mouth sought relief in hers.

A little later, she asked, "Why were you afraid? You must have guessed how I felt."

"In London, perhaps. I at least dreamed that I could make you love me if I tried. And I imagined that I would try...."

He smiled down at her. "You knew. I looked at you, and I knew that you knew that one day soon..."

"Yes," she whispered. "But you never did."

"Jamshid and I realized that Kavian was also seriously attracted to Alinor—we had to check her background. It was our duty. You were her close friend, you lived with her. We checked yours, too."

"Oh!"

"It was necessary. Either or both of you might have been in Kaljuk pay—anything was possible. I hated it, but my duty was plain.

"I remember the moment that I discovered who you were. Who your father was. I looked at the report, I read the name. And I—I saw it all in that moment, Lana. I saw that war would come, that it would take everything from us. I would have nothing to offer you, or any woman.

"And I told myself that you could never be mine."

She was silent, taking it in. "Did you love me then? The night that I—that we made love?"

"I loved you, then and always. I told myself I loved you too much to try to bind you to me when I had no future. I had promised myself, *if the king's negotiations go well, if it is not as I feared, I will return and find her*…but I could not resist you when you came of your own accord into my arms."

Feeling coursed through her at his words, melting her.

"Why didn't you leave me a note, some word?" she cried involuntarily, remembering that anguish.

He took a breath and his lips tightened behind the black beard.

"I thought—forgive me, Lana. I did not know you loved me. I thought you only knew that I loved you, and you gave yourself to me out of charity, the way a woman will when a man goes to war.

"I stood looking down at you as you slept, wanting to wake you, to say to you, come with me, and let us face whatever comes together. But in that moment, your father's wealth rose up before me, and I thought—*How fortunate, to fall in love with a wealthy woman on the eve of war!* And I turned away and left you there."

She sobbed once. "I wanted to come with you. I wanted to help you fight. I'd have done anything…I wrote you, I tried to tell you."

She saw him close his eyes. "I was a coward, disguising myself as a strong man. When I came home, my sister said it. She said that a man afraid of a woman's money was no better than a man who feared the sword, but I did not accept it...."

"And when the war ended, you never thought of looking me up?"

He shook his head. "Lana, when the war ended, I was here, in this room, wondering whether I would live or die. My father was dead, my brother dead, the estate in ruins. I did not then know that the Shield of Aram had gone, but my wound—I feared that the injury had made me infertile.

"I believed that everything had been taken from me, Lana, including the future. Why should I think of you then? I could not even promise you a child. I thought the al Khosravi line would die with me."

"I wish I had known," she whispered.

"I recovered and went back to Parvan and the work of recovery. And then, there you were, exactly as you had been, beautiful, vital, and now bursting with pity for my country and with a generosity that could scarcely be believed. You gave everything, and took nothing."

She bit her lip. "And you would accept nothing from me."

"A man does not become a dog at the table of the woman whom he loves," he said fiercely, and she looked nervously into his proud face and made the wise decision not to press that mystery further.

"You couldn't look at me without gritting your teeth. I thought you despised me."

"Despise you?" His hand tightened fiercely on her arm, so that she gasped in protest. "I did not despise you. I despised myself, for still loving a woman when I had nothing to offer her."

She wrapped her arms around his neck, drawing him

close. "You offer me everything," she whispered, and it was true. He gave her love, he gave her past, present and future, and she had none of those without him.

As if he had been holding himself in check, she was suddenly startled by the ferocity of passion that blazed in him. His hands tightened on her, his mouth came closer.

"I love you," he said. "Will you marry me, my love, my life?"

"If you give me the apricot orchard," she replied, a smile teasing the corners of her lips.

But he was beyond teasing now. His mouth covered hers with a hunger that made the world go black. His hand, tight on her arm, lifted her against him, his other hand held her head, the fingers threading through her curls.

He rolled over on his back, drawing her with him, wrapping her tightly in his arms as his kiss hungered, tasted, drank. His hand in her hair drew her head away as his lips trailed from the sensitive corner of her mouth and along her tender cheek to her ear, then down the line of her jaw and underneath, to where her quick heartbeat pulsed.

His lips found her throat, then trailed little hungry mouthings up the line of her neck to her chin, and so to her mouth again.

Then his hands released her, and moved to the buttons of the silky jacket. One by one, as she raised herself above him, he undid the buttons, his mouth following the opening with its wet heat, down the center of her chest until the two sides of the jacket parted.

Her bare stomach was against the heat of his; her hips, nestled in his, felt the pulse of his need. Her full round breasts swung free above him, and she whim pered her pleasure as his strong lips pressed the nipple and his tongue brushed it, over and over.

Then his hand moved up again to cup her head and draw her face down to his. His eyes searched hers, the deep wounded purple almost breaking her heart with love.

"Lana."

She was silent, gazing at him, still hardly able to accept the change that a few days had made in her heart, life, future.

"How handsome our sons will be," she murmured, her eyes stroking the broad white forehead, caressing the thick curl of black hair, the straight, serious eyebrows, the strong, narrow nose, firm lips, the curling beard.

"I hope they'll inherit your eyes. And the girls, too. Such a haunting colour. I used to dream of that colour.... That would be all I'd remember when I woke, just the colour. But I always knew it was a dream of you."

He kissed her hard. "Then we were together in our dreams, for I dreamt of you night after night on the battlefield."

She was entranced. "Truly?"

"It was as if at night, God sent me visions of you, to help me get through the days of war."

"Was it terrible, Arash?" she whispered.

"Terrible? Yes. If I had not had you there…there is a spring in the valley, in a protected place above the house, a spring of the freshest water, Lana. In the summer one bathes there, under the waterfall. Nowhere in the world is water so fresh, so pure, with such a taste.

"My dreams of you were like that water, as if my soul stood naked in a pure stream, and was refreshed."

She lifted her head and closed her eyes, breathing deep to calm her beating heart. "What did you dream?"

"Sometimes you waited for me, on a height, wearing white, and I struggled through forest or storm to reach you, and found peace. If I went to sleep thirsty your breasts flowed with milk or water into a cup, and I drank it and my thirst was quenched. If I was hungry you gave birth to peaches and offered them to me."

"Oh!"

"Yes, they were strong dreams, dreams of power. When I went to sleep tired, too tired even to sleep well, then you would come to me in a glow of sensual beauty, as you were that night, and you would say, *make love to me, Arash, make love to me,* and then strength would flood me, and I would love you, and the tiredness would be gone from my body in the morning."

He stroked her breast, cupped its weight in his palm, grazed the pad of his thumb over the tip.

"When I was wounded, you were there, too. Here," he corrected himself. "You were in this room. I opened my eyes and saw you, sitting by me. You said something to me, speaking very clearly, but afterwards I could not remember what it was...I knew only that it was required of me to fight and live.

"But mostly I dreamed of touching you," he said softly, suiting the action to the word, "of stroking your hair, your back, your thighs and breasts...and of you crying with pleasure. I dreamed of your face as it was that night, your mouth wide and your eyes squeezed tight, and my name on your tongue.

"Then I understood why women are generous with

men going to war. Because dreams and memories of that night—many times I had nothing else.''

She was too moved to speak, and for several minutes they looked silently, hungrily, into each other's face.

''I'm glad you had that,'' she murmured at last. ''But it definitely wasn't my conscious reason for what I did. I don't think I'd ever have guessed, even in my wildest moments of hoping that…''

''No? But perhaps you did not know everything that moved you. Perhaps you were nominated by God to give me what would keep me alive.''

She frowned as a jealous thought scratched her. ''But you would have remembered some other women if I hadn't listened to the call.''

In the warm shadows his eyes glowed deep, wet-velvet purple. ''Lana,'' he said. ''Have you not understood?''

She blinked. ''Understood?''

He drew down her head and kissed her. ''Lana,'' he murmured against her lips. ''There have been no other women for me. You are my first, my only love.''

Her breath rushed in in a long, audible gasp, and his arms encircled her naked back under the shirt as he pulled her down against him, her breasts flattening against the warm bare skin of his chest.

And then they were kissing with a renewal of that desperate urgency, a wild, hungry need of soul and body, that was half-tender, half-fierce. He pulled the black shirt down her arms and she eagerly dragged herself from its folds before moving her hands to the waist of his trousers to untie the drawstring….

Then at last they were naked, each open to the eyes and mouth and touch of the other, to the toying and kissing, the yearning and need.

And now there was nothing between them and love.

He lay on his side, facing her, one hand cupping her delicate head with fierce tenderness, his fingers in her curls, the purple of his eyes melting her like wax. Her own hand was against his face, and she felt her love pouring through her palm and into him.

"Make love to me, Arash," she whispered, in the old incantation. "Make love to me."

He lifted her thigh with one impatient hand, and drew it over his hip, opening her to him, and then he fitted his flesh to her, and cupped her hips, and thrust home.

The stroke melted them both with sudden, impossible heat, with wild delight, with a burning of love that fired up and consumed them. They thrust hungrily against each other, each searching for the truth of who they were, knowing that it could be found in the Other.

Drunk, wild, they cried aloud into each other's being their joy, their increasing need. He clasped her, held her, but he could not get deep enough into her self. He rolled onto his back, drawing her over him, and she obediently knelt above him, giving him the deepest access. Now his body went his full length in her, and she cried wildly as each driving thrust pounded against the door that had never been opened in her, in him.

Under his guiding, passionate hands she rose and fell on the pounding waves of a storm at sea, sensing the wild depths they rode, magic with unseen riches, unsounded, deep, dark, overwhelming.

They rose and fell as the storm built, lashing them, and high waves lifted dangerous over them and smashed down, so that they gasped and choked on pleasure, and cried in amazement.

Then, after endless time on the cruel swell, a wave

climbed steep and stark above them, and they sensed its presence and gasped for the air they would need. It thundered down against their frail human forms, potent, perilous, too strong against their humanness. Then they were washed under, rolling, twisting, calling, sobbing, as Love tore a path through them into what we call the world.

Then they understood both pleasure and pain—the joy of Union, the pain of knowing they could not sustain it for more than these few moments of blinding sensation that were love, and joy, and life, and Truth.

Fourteen

The heat of the desert soaked into their bodies, unravelling the strain of the past months and years. They rode Omar's horses into the desert, they swam in the swimming pool, they browsed in the souks of his city, where artisans engraved silver trays and cooks fried felafel, where charcoal sellers and apple growers offered their produce.

And always they escaped from the world back into the magic of his bedroom, where they loved, and toyed, and wept, and talked.

"Tell me how it was for you," she said once, and he told her how her body had thrilled him and troubled him, a young man going to a war from which he might never return, tasting a delight he might never know again, might never know but for her generosity....

"You were—twenty-two or three, weren't you?"

"I had just turned twenty-one."

"That's pretty old for a guy to be a virgin."

"In the West, it seems so. Not in the Valley of Aram. There it is still accepted that both a man and a woman will be virgin when they marry. We marry young—most girls are married by the age of twenty, men by twenty-two."

"Did your father and mother have someone picked out for you?"

"No, because it was understood from an early age that I would go to the palace and be named Cup Companion to Prince Kavian. And before that I must attend university."

"And you never met anyone at university?"

He smiled. "There was a girl, yes. But of course she expected to be virgin when she married. In Parvan this attitude is still common."

"And you never pushed her, never tried?"

"Not when I was not sure of wanting to marry her. If we had become engaged and the wedding could not take place immediately—then, perhaps. In Parvan a man does not lightly take from a woman what he can never restore to her."

"And then you came to England."

"Then I came, and I saw you, and I understood why I had not been sure of making Tahira my wife. With you doubt fell away, there was a certainty that nothing could hide from me."

"But—"

"But war threatened, and how could I in honour try to bind you to me when I could not see the future beyond it?"

"Well, I was bound to you anyway, so you might as well have."

When she spoke such things to him, he had no answer but a hungry kiss, and to draw her deep into drowning pleasure.

"Have you had a relaxing couple of days?" Jana asked.

They were on Prince Omar's private terrace, overlooking the swimming pool, the desert, the stars. A waiter was offering them flute glasses.

"Yes," was all Lana could say. She lifted a glass from the tray with a smile of thanks. "And how was your conference?"

"In some ways, fruitful." They chatted lightly, and without seeming to do so, Jana drew her friend aside, so that Lana found herself settled in a comfortable chair, out of earshot of the men.

"Everything has worked out, I see," Jana said with a smile.

Lana blinked. "Pardon me?"

"Between you and Arash. I see that things are finally settled. Are you—is it a formal engagement?" she went on, while Lana blinked at her, mouth open.

"Yes, but—"

Jana heaved a satisfied sigh. *"Alhamdolillah!* Oh, Alinor's going to be *very* pleased. She was so sure! Have you told her yet?"

"Jana, what—what on earth are you talking about?" Lana asked faintly.

"You didn't guess?"

"No! Guess what?"

"Well, you see, Alinor told me that she was sure you and Arash were…the way she put it was, you were both deliberately ignoring the obvious. So we plotted a little for a way to get you together, and that's when

I started to press you to come for a visit. And Alinor somehow arranged that Arash should be your escort.''

"It was all *plotted?*"

"Not the storm.'' Princess Jana laughed. "That was fate taking a hand, I guess.''

"Alinor never said a word to me.''

"She didn't want to put you on your guard. Whatever was keeping you two apart—well, she didn't think talk would fix it. Are you making the announcement right away? Can we call her tonight and tell her she was right?''

At the other end of the terrace, Omar lighted a black cigarette and blew out the smoke as he nodded his satisfaction at what his cousin had just told him.

"Congratulations. It's good to see you so happy, Arash. I suppose the two of you will go home as soon as possible, and start to put your estates in order.''

"Yes,'' said Arash.

"Your people have been too long without security. They need you there, they need to see you, too, rebuilding. To know that it is finally and definitely over.''

"Yes,'' said Arash. "I wasn't raised to it, the way Kamil was. I have too much to learn. But I guess they understand and will suffer through it with me.''

"Your presence is the most important part of the equation. If you'll take advice from me...''

"I'll be very grateful for advice from you.''

"Then I suggest you don't wait any longer to get the Shield of Aram back into the valley, where they can see it. I know the house is pretty badly damaged, but they need to know it's there. I understand the *majlis* is still standing?''

Arash's lips compressed. "Omar, that's the worst part—"

"It's still in its protective packaging. I never saw any reason to unwrap it, but if you'd like to do so to be sure it's in good condition before taking it back, it'll be easy enough. The other pieces your father...Arash, what—?"

The flute glass had smashed into a hundred tiny fragments on the beautiful tiles. Arash pressed a hand on the stone balustrade, needing its reality.

"Sorry, Omar, did I drop my—*what did you say?*"

A servant was already brushing up the shards. Omar grasped his cousin's arm above the elbow.

"What is it, Arash?"

"*You* have the Shield of Aram?"

"Of course I have the Shield of Aram. And the other treasures your father sent to me for safekeeping. Did you imagine I had sold them?"

"Omar—*Allah!* Can this be true? I thought it lost—stolen!"

There was a long pregnant pause as each cousin assimilated what the other had said.

Omar spoke first. "Your father did not tell you? Not after Kamil was killed? Kamil certainly knew."

"I hardly spoke to him, all through the war. When did he send it?"

"About a year before the end of the war, at a time when the bombing had intensified. He had sent things here that were to be sold—we thought my agents would get the best price. At that time he sent all that remained, including the shield. We did it with night helicopter flights.

"Some of these treasures your father had earmarked to be held as long as possible, to be the last sold. They were the most precious, for reasons both of tradition and monetary value. He said that if they outlasted the war, either they could be sold to fund the rebuilding, or be restored to their place, depending. Many of those did survive, and are here in my treasury. Did you know nothing of this?''

''Nothing. I knew he had sent them out for sale, of course. The shield I believed lost. I thought everything gone.''

''I am glad to be bearer of such welcome news. Shall we go to the gallery now, so that you can see what is still in your possession?''

Arash blinked, his brain still reeling. ''Shall—'' Arash shook his head, trying to clear it, without success. He gestured towards the servant who appeared to summon them to the table.

''If your chef won't object to a delay—''

''To hell with my chef,'' said Omar.

''Oh my, is that *it?* Oh, how magnificent!'' Lana cried softly, as, under Arash's hands, the last of the protective covering was lifted away and the Shield of Aram was revealed.

They stood together in the cleaned, restored *majlis,* which sparkled with polish and new paint. Behind them the door was open on a rich late-spring day.

Outside, on the slopes, the sun burnished leaves and flowers, the wings of foraging bees and butterflies, the pelts of skittish horses, the sparkle of stones and springs, and the mighty rush of the waterfall.

Everywhere workmen sawed and plastered, men laid bricks, artists worked, artisans crafted and fitted and polished. Ploughmen worked the fields, and gardeners toiled among the trees and flowers. Further along the valley a thousand saplings waited to be placed in the dark, nourishing soil where the last of the blackened skeletons of their predecessors were being lifted out.

Inside the *majlis,* with a powerful heave, the sheikh of the tribe of Aram lifted the great shield of his people and restored it to its home on the wall of the place where for centuries his ancestors had advised and been advised by the people of his valley.

It glowed with deep power in the rays of the sun, blinding with its flashes of gold and silver, the ruby at its centre pulsing with deep, mysterious light that held the eye in a hypnotic grip.

He stepped back with only a faint trace of a limp now, and put his arm around his wife-to-be, and together they gazed at the symbol of good fortune and right guidance for them, and the valley and its inhabitants.

"It feels so right, Arash," Lana murmured, because she could find no better words. She turned to him. "I understand now."

He nodded. "Tomorrow," he said, "you take me for your husband here."

"Yes," she said firmly.

"You are not afraid?"

"I'm nervous, but not afraid." Unconsciously she touched her stomach, where the tiny seed of their union already nestled. "Anyway, it's a bit late for second thoughts!"

Sheikh Arash Durrani ibn Zahir al Khosravi turned and wrapped his love in the circle of his arms.

"Yes," he agreed, gazing down at her. "We will no longer look back. Now is the time for looking forward, my temptation and my delight. Now we face the future, and we face it together. You and I, and the child, and our people.''

*   *   *   *   *

Watch for talented author
Alexandra Sellers's next sensual
romance and discover how Jalal,
the mysterious bandit featured in

BELOVED SHEIKH,

finds forever love in his own story—

SHEIKH'S HONOR,
on sale May 2000

and available only
from Silhouette Desire.

If you enjoyed what you just read,
then we've got an offer you can't resist!

Take 2 bestselling love stories FREE!

Plus get a FREE surprise gift!

Clip this page and mail it to Silhouette Reader Service™

IN U.S.A.
3010 Walden Ave.
P.O. Box 1867
Buffalo, N.Y. 14240-1867

IN CANADA
P.O. Box 609
Fort Erie, Ontario
L2A 5X3

YES! Please send me 2 free Silhouette Desire® novels and my free surprise gift. Then send me 6 brand-new novels every month, which I will receive months before they're available in stores. In the U.S.A., bill me at the bargain price of $3.12 plus 25¢ delivery per book and applicable sales tax, if any*. In Canada, bill me at the bargain price of $3.49 plus 25¢ delivery per book and applicable taxes**. That's the complete price and a savings of over 10% off the cover prices—what a great deal! I understand that accepting the 2 free books and gift places me under no obligation ever to buy any books. I can always return a shipment and cancel at any time. Even if I never buy another book from Silhouette, the 2 free books and gift are mine to keep forever. So why not take us up on our invitation. You'll be glad you did!

225 SEN CNFA
326 SEN CNFC

Name	(PLEASE PRINT)	
Address	Apt.#	
City	State/Prov.	Zip/Postal Code

* Terms and prices subject to change without notice. Sales tax applicable in N.Y.
** Canadian residents will be charged applicable provincial taxes and GST.
   All orders subject to approval. Offer limited to one per household.
   ® are registered trademarks of Harlequin Enterprises Limited.

DES99   ©1998 Harlequin Enterprises Limited

SILHOUETTE'S 20TH ANNIVERSARY CONTEST
OFFICIAL RULES
NO PURCHASE NECESSARY TO ENTER

1. To enter, follow directions published in the offer to which you are responding. Contest begins 1/1/00 and ends on 8/24/00 (the "Promotion Period"). Method of entry may vary. Mailed entries must be postmarked by 8/24/00, and received by 8/31/00.

2. During the Promotion Period, the Contest may be presented via the Internet. Entry via the Internet may be restricted to residents of certain geographic areas that are disclosed on the Web site. To enter via the Internet, if you are a resident of a geographic area in which Internet entry is permissible, follow the directions displayed on-line, including typing your essay of 100 words or fewer telling us "Where In The World Your Love Will Come Alive." On-line entries must be received by 11:59 p.m. Eastern Standard time on 8/24/00. Limit one e-mail entry per person, household and e-mail address per day, per presentation. If you are a resident of a geographic area in which entry via the Internet is permissible, you may, in lieu of submitting an entry on-line, enter by mail, by hand-printing your name, address, telephone number and contest number/name on an 8"x 11" plain piece of paper and telling us in 100 words or fewer "Where In The World Your Love Will Come Alive," and mailing via first-class mail to: Silhouette 20th Anniversary Contest, (in the U.S.) P.O. Box 9069, Buffalo, NY 14269-9069; (In Canada) P.O. Box 637, Fort Erie, Ontario, Canada L2A 5X3. Limit one 8"x 11" mailed entry per person, household and e-mail address per day. <u>On-line and/or 8"x 11" mailed entries received from persons residing in geographic areas in which Internet entry is not permissible will be disqualified.</u> No liability is assumed for lost, late, incomplete, inaccurate, nondelivered or misdirected mail, or misdirected e-mail, for technical, hardware or software failures of any kind, lost or unavailable network connection, or failed, incomplete, garbled or delayed computer transmission or any human error which may occur in the receipt or processing of the entries in the contest.

3. Essays will be judged by a panel of members of the Silhouette editorial and marketing staff based on the following criteria:

> Sincerity (believability, credibility)—50%
> Originality (freshness, creativity)—30%
> Aptness (appropriateness to contest ideas)—20%

Purchase or acceptance of a product offer does not improve your chances of winning. In the event of a tie, duplicate prizes will be awarded.

4. All entries become the property of Harlequin Enterprises Ltd., and will not be returned. Winner will be determined no later than 10/31/00 and will be notified by mail. Grand Prize winner will be required to sign and return Affidavit of Eligibility within 15 days of receipt of notification. Noncompliance within the time period may result in disqualification and an alternative winner may be selected. All municipal, provincial, federal, state and local laws and regulations apply. Contest open only to residents of the U.S. and Canada who are 18 years of age or older, and is void wherever prohibited by law. Internet entry is restricted solely to residents of those geographical areas in which Internet entry is permissible. Employees of Torstar Corp., their affiliates, agents and members of their immediate families are not eligible. Taxes on the prizes are the sole responsibility of winners. Entry and acceptance of any prize offered constitutes permission to use winner's name, photograph or other likeness for the purposes of advertising, trade and promotion on behalf of Torstar Corp. without further compensation to the winner, unless prohibited by law. Torstar Corp and D.L. Blair, Inc., their parents, affiliates and subsidiaries, are not responsible for errors in printing or electronic presentation of contest or entries. In the event of printing or other errors which may result in unintended prize values or duplication of prizes, all affected contest materials or entries shall be null and void. If for any reason the Internet portion of the contest is not capable of running as planned, including infection by computer virus, bugs, tampering, unauthorized intervention, fraud, technical failures, or any other causes beyond the control of Torstar Corp. which corrupt or affect the administration, secrecy, fairness, integrity or proper conduct of the contest, Torstar Corp. reserves the right, at its sole discretion, to disqualify any individual who tampers with the entry process and to cancel, terminate, modify or suspend the contest or the Internet portion thereof. In the event of a dispute regarding an on-line entry, the entry will be deemed submitted by the authorized holder of the e-mail account submitted at the time of entry. Authorized account holder is defined as the natural person who is assigned to an e-mail address by an Internet access provider, on-line service provider or other organization that is responsible for arranging e-mail address for the domain associated with the submitted e-mail address.

5. Prizes: Grand Prize—a $10,000 vacation to anywhere in the world. Travelers (at least one must be 18 years of age or older) or parent or guardian if one traveler is a minor, must sign and return a Release of Liability prior to departure. Travel must be completed by December 31, 2001, and is subject to space and accommodations availability. Two hundred (200) Second Prizes—a two-book limited edition autographed collector set from one of the Silhouette Anniversary authors: Nora Roberts, Diana Palmer, Linda Howard or Annette Broadrick (value $10.00 each set). All prizes are valued in U.S. dollars.

6. For a list of winners (available after 10/31/00), send a self-addressed, stamped envelope to: Harlequin Silhouette 20th Anniversary Winners, P.O. Box 4200, Blair, NE 68009-4200.

Contest sponsored by Torstar Corp., P.O. Box 9042, Buffalo, NY 14269-9042.

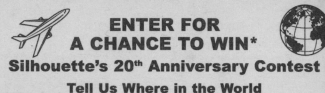

ENTER FOR
A CHANCE TO WIN*

Silhouette's 20th Anniversary Contest

Tell Us Where in the World
You Would Like *Your* Love To Come Alive...
And We'll Send the Lucky Winner There!

Silhouette wants to take you wherever
your happy ending can come true.

Here's how to enter: Tell us, in 100 words or less,
where you want to go to make your love come alive!

In addition to the grand prize, there will be 200
runner-up prizes, collector's-edition book sets
autographed by one of the Silhouette anniversary
authors: **Nora Roberts, Diana Palmer,
Linda Howard** or **Annette Broadrick**.

DON'T MISS YOUR CHANCE TO WIN!
ENTER NOW! No Purchase Necessary

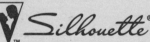

Silhouette®
Where love comes alive™

Name:

Address:

City: State/Province:

Zip/Postal Code:

Mail to Harlequin Books: **In the U.S.**: P.O. Box 9069, Buffalo, NY
14269-9069; **In Canada**: P.O. Box 637, Fort Erie, Ontario, L4A 5X3

*No purchase necessary—for contest details send a self-addressed stamped envelope to:
Silhouette's 20th Anniversary Contest, P.O. Box 9069, Buffalo, NY, 14269-9069 (include
contest name on self-addressed envelope). Residents of Washington and Vermont may
omit postage. Open to Cdn. (excluding Quebec) and U.S. residents who are 18 or over.
Void where prohibited. Contest ends August 31, 2000.

PS20CON_R